BROKEN DREAMS

A CHRISTIAN MEDICAL ROMANCE

MONROE FAMILY

LAURA SCOTT

PROLOGUE

As she walked into her apartment her cell phone rang. Amber Monroe inwardly groaned. Was someone from the hospital calling already? Had something happened to one of her patients? Concern had her stopping midstride and fishing in her bag for her cell phone. When she saw her brother's name she answered in surprise.

"Adam? Is something wrong?"

Silence. Alarm skittered across her nerves.

"Mom? Dad?" She forced the questions through her tight throat.

"No, our parents are fine." His reassuring words made her relax.

"What then? I just walked in from work." She sighed. "It was a rough day."

"It's Shane, Amber. He...there was a horrible accident—a plane crash in the mountains near Beijing and I'm so sorry. He didn't make it."

Dazed she sank onto the nearest chair. Shane? Dead? This couldn't be happening. There had to be some mistake. Shane was too young, only thirty-three, he couldn't possibly be dead. She shook her head, wanting to scream in protest, but Adam's heavy silence held her in check. She'd known Shane Reinhart her entire life, mostly because Shane was Adam's best friend. For years, her parents treated Shane as if he were part of their family.

One day, she'd hoped to marry him, making Shane a member of the family for good.

"I'm sorry for you, too, Adam." She forced herself to push beyond her own grief to consider what her brother was going through. "Are you going to be alright?"

"Yeah." He didn't sound convincing. "I still need to let Mom and Dad know."

"I'll be right over." No way was she letting Adam tell her parents alone.

"Thanks, Amber." Her brother sounded old. Tired.

She set her phone on the table, then buried her face in her hands allowing the keening sorrow and tears to come.

Her relationship with Shane had only just grown beyond the friendship stage. But now he was gone.

Forever.

CHAPTER ONE

Four months later...

"Come on, Mr. Goetz, you're almost there." Amber encouraged the older man who leaned heavily on his walker as he made his way slowly, painfully, down the hall to the community dining room at the Veteran's hospital's rehabilitation center.

"Bah, I ain't almost there." The stodgy old man scowled and set his walker down on the linoleum floor then shuffled his feet to catch up. "I don't know why you don't let me eat in my room."

She couldn't help but smile. "Because I care too much about you to allow you to wallow in misery all alone, that's why. Look at the bright sunlight pouring through the windows. It's a beautiful day."

One rubber foot of his walker stuck to the floor and he lost his balance, leaning heavily to his left side. His weak side, thanks to the broken hip he'd sustained. His rehab stay was to strengthen the weaker muscles in his left leg, making sure he could perform activities of daily living.

"It's all right. I have you." She quickly tightened the

muscles of her arm beneath his supporting his weight the best she could while hanging on to the walker to keep it from toppling over. After a few tense minutes, Mr. Goetz managed to get his left leg steadied beneath him and slowly shifted his weight so that it was equally distributed.

Still, she didn't loosen her grip on his arm or the walker. "Are you all right Mr. Goetz? I promise, I won't let you go until you're feeling steady."

"Yeah, yeah. I got it." The near collision with the floor eased some of his crustiness. "I can make it."

"I know you can," she assured him. "You're getting stronger. And I'll be right here with you the entire way."

The tangy scent of tomato and basil filled the air as they drew closer to the dining room. Another two steps and he managed to get into position to sit down at the table where three other men waited. Without any help, he eased into his seat.

"You did great, Mr. Goetz." She moved his walker out of the way, but not out of his reach. She patted his arm. "I'm proud of you."

"You're a sweetheart." Despite his earlier protests, his scowl eased into a smile. Being near his cronies had already brightened his spirits. Which was exactly why she'd pushed the issue of his coming to the dining room for his meals. "When are you going to marry me, Amber Monroe?"

She laughed. His proposal was as regular as the noon-time meal. "Mr. Goetz, you know my answer hasn't changed. I can't marry you, or anyone," she added, sternly eyeing the other men seated at the table who often joined in with their own proposals. "Until I've met my goal of traveling to all fifty states."

"Huh. What's so great about wanting to leave here?"

Mr. Sutherland asked. "We all signed the petition so you would stay."

She barely refrained from rolling her eyes. "I'm not leaving for another five weeks, Mr. Sutherland, so relax. Chances are you'll be home long before then. And please, stop signing petitions. This is my choice, not the Veteran's hospital's decision.

"Amber?" One of the nurses gestured from the main desk. "Doctor Roland is on the phone."

"Don't let him hang up. I'll be right there." She had paged the physical medicine specialist four times since the start of her shift to discuss Mr. Goetz's care. She forced a smile. "Enjoy your meal, gentleman. And remember, behave."

"Aw, what fun is that?" Mr. Baker asked in a plaintive tone.

She laughed and shook her head as she left the dining room. Reaching over the desk, she pushed the blinking light on the multi-button phone. "Dr. Roland? I've been calling you all morning."

"I'm busy."

She should have known he wouldn't apologize and bit her tongue, forcing herself to concentrate on the matter at hand. "The results of the urine sample we sent yesterday on Harold Goetz indicate he has another urinary tract infection. I'm concerned about him. I'm not sure why we can't seem to clear this infection up."

"Give him ten days of double strength Bactrim. Is that all?" His dismissive tone infuriated her. He acted as if he didn't care if Mr. Goetz ever recovered from his infection.

"I don't know. Are you going to bother calling back the next time I page you?"

There was a moment of silence, then Dr. Roland

erupted. "Don't tell me how to run my unit. I always return my pages and don't you dare to insinuate otherwise." He slammed the phone in her ear.

Ouch. Amber winced and hung up. Apparently the truth hurts.

Irene one of her nurse colleagues on the unit stared at her with wide eyes. "I can't believe you said that to him."

"Yeah, well, I'm tired of him not answering our pages." She sighed and came around the desk to enter the telephone order into the computer. "If Roland ever made rounds, he'd know these things for himself, wouldn't he?" Irene nodded in agreement, so she continued, "He hasn't shown his face around here for three days, at least not on day shift and not in the evenings either, based on the lack of documentation in the patient's charts."

"I know. But still. I can't believe you actually said that to him." Irene was a newer graduate nurse, three years younger than Amber. Although it was at times like this that Amber felt as if she were one hundred years older. "What if he complains to our boss about you?"

"Let him." She shrugged even though she knew Roland could cause trouble for her if he wanted to. Despite being absent more often than not, Dr. Roland was still the medical director of the physical medicine rehab unit. Dealing with him was one of those things she wouldn't miss when she left to take her traveling nurse position in Florida. Although she was worried about what would happen to her patients when she was gone. If she didn't blow the whistle and stand up to keep Roland in line, who would?

"Do me a favor. Watch for the extra strength Bactrim that should be coming up from the pharmacy. Oh, and keep an eye on our patients. I'd better find Leanne and let her know my side of the story before Roland gets to her."

Irene let out a heavy sigh. "Okay, but if she asks me, I'll have to tell her the truth about what I overheard you say."

"Don't worry, I would never ask you to lie for me." She met Irene's gaze straight on. "I'll tell her exactly what I said, along with the fact that he hasn't made rounds in three days. I'm pretty sure there are rules about that."

"Good luck," Irene said.

She flashed a grim smile. Considering she'd already given her notice and her last day of employment was August 15th, she didn't really care if her boss fired her. Well, that wasn't entirely true. She'd never been fired from a job in her life, and honestly didn't really want to start now. Thankfully, she had nearly enough vacation time to cover the gap if necessary.

Maybe getting canned wouldn't be the worst thing, she thought knocking on the nursing director's office door. She wouldn't mind some time off. Even though she'd miss her patients.

Three hours later the end of her shift came all too quickly. There were never enough hours in the day to get the work finished. Instead of firing her, Leanne made her sign up for an educational session about positive communication between colleagues. She was glad her boss hadn't been too upset, and Leanne had promised to follow up with the chief of staff about Roland's lack of making rounds. As she headed home, she debated whether or not the chief of staff would take their concerns seriously or brush them off. Surely she couldn't be the first nurse to complain about the guy.

It bugged her that Roland was getting paid for taking care of his patients from the comfort of his chair on the other end of a phone rather than in person, using an actual stethoscope to do his own assessments.

She brushed off the annoyance. Roland wouldn't be her problem for much longer. The summer day was warm but not too hot as she walked the short six blocks home to her parent's house. She rolled her shoulders hoping to ease the nagging ache. Grabbing Mr. Goetz so he didn't fall had strained the muscles in her upper back. Again.

But she didn't dare complain not when she had to go home and help lift her incapacitated mother in and out of the bathtub. She winced, immediately ashamed of the selfish thought.

Shane's death had taken a toll on their whole family. Amber had grieved for what would never be. But then she'd decided this was the perfect time to break loose from her family. To take the first step in her dream of seeing the world. She'd always wanted to travel but losing Shane had been hard. Then, her mother had tripped over their dog Murphy, and had fallen down the stairs.

Her mom's broken hip was healing slowly but surely. Her dad watched over her mother while Amber was at work, but he couldn't do everything himself. At least her mother's hip fracture was on the mend. Soon her mom wouldn't need help at all.

Her parents had been upset by her decision to leave home and travel, but she couldn't let her love for them sway her from her goal. Her dream of marrying Shane had been broken, but she knew it was time to look ahead. She'd lived vicariously through her older siblings for years. It was time for her to do something for herself. She missed having her own apartment, having been forced to move back home after her mother had broken her hip. There were also five other Monroe siblings to keep an eye on her parents, while she was gone. Well, really only three, since Austin was in California and Aaron was in Boston.

Once she'd planned to travel with Shane. Her heart squeezed painfully in her chest. She'd known him her whole life, and just before he'd left for China, he'd kissed her, finally giving her a hint he was ready to take the relationship to the next level. Waiting for Shane to return home had been pure agony. Still, she hadn't blamed him for jumping at the chance to participate in a special surgical training program in Beijing. She would have done the same thing in his shoes.

Losing him felt surreal. Any minute, she expected him to vault onto the porch of her parent's house, demanding to know what was for dinner.

A heavy ache settled in her heart. She missed him.

As she approached her childhood home, she noticed a man with a cane standing near the mailbox. She estimated him to be in his early thirties, and he stood staring at the house thoughtfully. He was tall, at least six feet, his back ramrod straight and his dark hair cut military short. For a moment she wondered if he was a lost soldier looking for the veteran's hospital, even though he was dressed in worn jeans and T-shirt rather than a uniform.

He didn't seem to notice her until she was right next to him. With a polite smile, she greeted him. "Hello, may I help you? Are you lost?"

"Not lost, exactly. I believe this might be the Monroe house. I'm looking for Amber Monroe."

Her eyes widened. She'd never seen this stranger before in her life. "I'm Amber Monroe."

"Oh." He frowned, trailing his gaze over her. "I expected someone older."

She bit back a flash of impatience. She was twenty-six, not sixteen, and more than a little tired of people assuming the latter. It was humiliating the way she got carded when she went out with her coworkers, making her aware she looked younger than she was. "Well, I'm not expecting you." She scowled. "Are you sure you're looking for me?"

"Yes." Belatedly she noticed a dark blue duffel bag on the ground at his feet. He leaned down and carefully extracted a small, battered cardboard box. His facial expression didn't change as he straightened, but she sensed he was in excruciating pain the way each movement was slow and deliberate. With the solemn expression, he held out the box. "I have something that belongs to you. I'm sorry it took me so long to bring this, I was—unavoidably detained."

She didn't know who this guy was, and she was too tired to care. Crossing her arms over her chest, she silently refused his dubious offering. "Who are you? Why would you have anything that belongs to me?"

"My name is Nick Tanner, a friend and colleague of Shane Reinhart. This box contains letters and e-mail messages you sent during the time we were both on a six-month surgical training stint in Beijing." A tick spasmed in his cheek and his tone revealed no emotion as he added, "I'm very sorry for your loss."

NICK HOPED she'd take the stupid box before he made a fool of himself by falling flat on his face. Every muscle in his leg screamed in agony. The bright sunlight beating down on his bare head echoed the throbbing in his thigh and sweat beaded on his upper lip.

Shane's girlfriend finally took the cardboard box from his hands. His arm dropped to his side and he nearly closed his eyes in relief. He had overtaxed his injured muscles by traveling halfway across the country without the help of pain meds.

"Are you okay?" The girl who looked all of eighteen with her strawberry blonde hair pulled into a ponytail and the sprinkling of freckles across her nose, leaned toward him. A frown marred her pretty brow. "You look like you need to sit down."

He must be losing his touch. He could have sworn he hadn't revealed any sign of his pain. Nick forced himself to look into the girl's concerned blue eyes. "I'm fine. I don't need to sit down."

"Yeah." She scoffed. "Look, Mr. Tanner, I'm a nurse and I know for a fact you need to sit before you fall." She gestured to the steps leading to a wide porch in front of an old white farmhouse. "There's some shade from the sun over here."

Despite his determination to get out of there, he found himself walking stiffly toward the proffered shade. "Dr. Tanner."

"Excuse me?" She set the cardboard box beside her as she settled on the top step. A large Irish setter came bounding out the door waking his tail and greeting.

Idly, he reached out to pet the friendly dog, before bending awkwardly to take a seat on the steps beside her. "Never mind, call me Nick." Taking the weight off his leg brought immeasurable relief. Forgetting his resolve of not letting on how much he was hurting, he used his good hand to massage the tense muscles.

"Nick. Of course." He almost smiled when she tapped her temple with her index finger. "I remember now. Shane mentioned you in several of his letters and during our video calls. You're a trauma surgeon too, aren't you?"

The hint of smile faded. Shane. He had to remember

why he was here. To pay his respects to Shane's girlfriend. Mentally bracing himself, he turned so he could face her. "I was."

"But not anymore?"

He swallowed hard and shook his head. "Not exactly." Without thinking, he opened and closed his injured hand into a fist. His arm was coming along much better than his leg, but he was so far from being well, he couldn't imagine setting foot in an operating room. "At the moment, I'm more of a patient than a doctor."

"Hmm." Despite the strawberry blonde hair and freckles he suspected those intense blue eyes of hers didn't miss a thing. "And you came all this way to Milwaukee, Wisconsin, to give me a cardboard box filled with letters, messages and mementos I sent to Shane?"

"Yes." He had a strong desire to tell her the rest to explain everything, but the words stuck in his throat. The truth was his burden to bear. Nothing good would come of telling Shane's girlfriend what he knew.

Shane Reinhart's death was his fault.

CHAPTER TWO

A little girl with blonde pigtails ran out of the house, banging the screen door behind her. "Aunt Amber, Grandma wants to know what's taking you so long." Her eyes rounded with shocked surprise when she saw Nick sitting there. "Aunt Amber! Don't you know you're not supposed to talk to strangers?"

"Yes, Beth. But Dr. Tanner isn't a stranger, he's a friend." Nick almost smiled at how Amber stretched the truth for the child's benefit. "Tell Grandma I'll be in soon."

"Okay." The little girl spun like a top and dashed inside.

With an apologetic glance at him, she said, "Mom broke her hip a month ago and she needs help getting around."

And that was his cue to leave. He managed a smile. "Shane mentioned how the Monroe family was closer to him than his own. I can certainly see why he felt that way. Please, give your parents my regards."

"Why don't you stay for dinner?" Amber stood with a fluid movement he sorely envied. "My brother Adam will be here. He was a good friend of Shane's. I'm sure he'd love to talk to you."

Sucking in a deep breath to ward off the anticipated pain, he pushed himself to a standing position. A dark red hot jolt of pain flashed before his eyes, momentarily blinding him. Wow, something as easy as standing shouldn't be so difficult. To distract himself from his weakness, he focused his gaze on Amber's youthful face as he recited her sibling's names. "Aaron, Adam, Alec, Austin, and Amber. Don't tell me, let me guess. You guys are the A-team.

Amber laughed, the simple motion lit up her whole face, making him suck in another quick breath. "What can I say? My parents have a strange sense of humor. You forgot my sister, Andrea, she's between Aaron and Adam. Beth is her daughter. I have the dubious privilege of being the youngest. My sister has carried on the tradition, her children are Bethany and Benjamin. We can only pray she doesn't have four more. I'm not sure our family gatherings could take the noise."

He thought her family sounded wonderful. He'd heard bits and pieces about the Monroe family from Shane. Guilt over his death returned in full force. "You're very fortunate to have such a large family."

Her expression softened. "Yes, I know."

"Amber?" A booming male voice came from inside the house. "Beth tells us your boyfriend is here. Why don't you invite him in?" As he spoke, her father opened the door and stepped out on the porch. "You know your friends are always welcome. Hi. My name is Abe Monroe. My wife, Alice is inside." Her dad held out his hand. "Pleased to meet you."

"Nick Tanner, and it's nice to meet you too." Nick shook Amber's father's hand, subtly shifting his weight to ease the pain in his left leg before it buckled and he embarrassed himself by doing an ungainly nose dive off the side of the porch.

"Nick is Shane's friend." Amber rolled her eyes at her dad's assumption they were seeing each other. "He's a surgeon too, and was training with Shane over in Beijing. I just invited him to stay for dinner." She glanced over her shoulder while opening the door. "Dad, talk him into staying, while I run up to check on Mom."

"Really?" The older man's eyes brightened with keen interest as he gazed at Nick. Amber grinned slyly as she left him alone with her father. "You were with Shane in Beijing? I'd love to hear about your time there, if you don't mind."

Nick could swear he heard the clang of a jail door slamming shut behind him. How was he going to get out of this? For a moment, he considered simply walking away. But then realized he owed the Monroe clan more than a couple of minutes of his time. Shane had called them his surrogate family. So what if he didn't have his pain meds and muscle relaxants with him? They didn't work all that well anyway. He could suffer a few more hours.

To be honest, he didn't have anywhere else to go. Except back to an empty motel room. For years he'd roamed the world thriving on his independence. But since his accident he'd become keenly aware of his lack of a home. Of a family.

"No, sir, I don't mind at all." He forced a smile. "I'd love to stay for dinner."

"Great! Come on in." Abe gave a hearty laugh and opened the door gesturing for Nick to follow. "I'll tell Andrea to set another place at the table."

He followed Amber's father inside the house and immediately felt surrounded by the warmth of the Monroe family. One entire wall of the living room was covered with framed pictures of the children, including he saw with a grimace, several pictures including Shane.

And of course, dozens of Amber.

In his humble opinion, she was the cutest of the bunch.

He felt like a traitor stepping into this wholesome homestead. When he heard the tinkling sound of Amber's laughter, he knew he was sunk.

His mission of returning the cardboard box to Amber had been completed. He had no intention of telling the family the graphic details about the plane crash that had nearly killed him and had stolen Shane's life. The hotel had sent his bags to the hospital upon his transfer back to the United States, but had mixed up some of his and Shane's belongings. He wasn't even sure how it happened, some phrase had caught his eye and he ended up reading part of a letter. Then another. Then all of them. Every letter and email Amber had sent to Shane.

Then he'd suffered complications from surgery that had extended his stay in the hospital for another two months. If he was brutally honest, Amber's letters were the only thing that kept him from losing his mind during the long, painful weeks of rehab. He'd read each letter and e-mail so often he could quote them by memory.

Bad enough he'd betrayed her privacy. What was he doing hanging around here?

Meeting Amber in person hadn't helped exorcise his demons. In fact, just the opposite. Now that he'd met her in person, he only wanted to stay.

AMBER COULDN'T CONCENTRATE on taking care of her mother, not when she could hear the rumble of Nick's deep voice downstairs as he spoke to her family. She was more than a little intrigued by the tall, dark-haired stranger.

Although he really wasn't a stranger, she silently corrected. That hadn't been just a line to satisfy her niece. Shane had mentioned Nick several times in his letters, how they'd go out and play tourist in Beijing after putting in long grueling hours in the operating room. Shane had also been impressed by Nick's skill as a surgeon. It was such a shame he'd been injured.

"Ouch!" Her mother yelped.

"Oh, I'm so sorry." She winced and turned her attention back to the task of getting her mother out of the bathtub. "I didn't mean to bump your knee like that. Here, wrap your arm around my shoulder so I can support your weight off your hip."

"That's all right, dear." Her mother flashed a forgiving smile. "Did you have a rough day at work?"

"No more than usual." With caution, she helped her mother stand then step out of the bathtub. According to the physical therapists, they weren't supposed to rely on the automatic lift anymore, even though her mother preferred the ease of using the supportive equipment.

"I'm falling," her mother cried, waving her arm in panic.

"Don't worry I have you." She spoke in a soothing tone and tightened her grip on her mother's tiny frame. Thankfully her mother was small boned and didn't weigh very much. "You're doing great, Mom. A few more weeks and you'll be getting in and out of the tub on your own."

"I'm not so sure about that." Her mom dropped into the chair with a sigh. "Maybe you should put off leaving for another couple of months. You know, Andrea could help use your help with the kids once in a while with her husband away on his business trips."

Amber bit back the automatic protest. She knew her mother wasn't trying to make her feel guilty. But the end result was a pretty impressive guilt trip, just the same. She managed a smile. "Here, let's get you dressed. We have a guest for dinner."

"Really?" Her mother perked up, diverted by the prospect of company, as she had hoped. "Who?"

"Dr. Nick Tanner. He's a friend of Shane's." She wrapped her mother in a large bath towel. "Let's get you into the bedroom and you can tell me what you'd like to wear."

"A friend of Shane's?" Her mother used the walker to make her way from the bathroom into the bedroom. "Oh my."

Oh my, was right. Her impression exactly, she thought with a wry grin. Men had not been high on her list of priorities after Shane's passing. Yet she wouldn't be a female if she hadn't noticed the extremely handsome Nick Tanner.

Not that she was interested in anything except hearing about his travels. Her pulse quickened at the thought. Beijing! How she'd longed to see the Forbidden City in the Ming Tombs that Shade had described in his letters. She could just imagine what it must have been like to travel through a country where you couldn't speak the language. For too long now, she lived vicariously through others.

Six more weeks and she'd start her traveling nurse assignment. She'd be happy to at least see the breadth of the United States, but she'd already begun to save money to travel overseas as well.

Her feet itched to shake off the Wisconsin dust once and for all. Not that she wouldn't return home for visits.

Yet, as the youngest, she'd been forced to wait as one by one her siblings and of course, Shane, had taken off for adventures unknown.

Andrea had come back once since she decided to marry Stuart, and still Amber hadn't managed to find her way across state lines. First she'd needed enough nursing experience to qualify for a traveling nurse assignment. Then Shane's death, followed by her mother's broken hip, had postponed her plans. She hadn't minded helping out. But now, it seemed as if her family was determined she should never leave. As much as she loved them, they'd keep trying to run her life, refusing to believe she was capable of surviving on her own.

As far as she was concerned, she'd be just fine without them. She longed to get away. She could practically taste the spicy southern cuisine, feel the salty spray on her face as she stood on the sandy shores of the Gulf of Mexico.

Her heart raced with anticipation. She could hardly wait.

AMBER LISTENED in awe as Nick described his and Shane's trip to the Great Wall of China. She imagined how the winding wall must have looked, zig zagging like a snake through the green, hilly mountains. Suddenly, moving to Florida sounded far too tame.

Maybe she needed to reconsider her initial goal of seeing all fifty states. There would always be plenty of time to travel her homeland, but going overseas now, while she was young enough to explore the sights, sounded like a much better plan. Were there traveling nurse assignments available overseas? How different could the nurse's responsibilities be? She thought about some of the European medical articles she'd read and inwardly grimaced. Even some routine medical phrases different, and she had to assume the duties were, too.

Maybe that wasn't such a good idea after all.

"Thanks for dinner." Nick's voice interrupted her thoughts. "I very much enjoyed the home cooked meal." Her sister, Andrea, preened at his praise. "But I really need to get going."

Amber could tell her father was disappointed, but he gave in gracefully. "Of course you do. How long will you be in town?"

"I'm not sure, probably only a few days." Nick flashed an apologetic smile. "If I have time, I'll stop back before I leave."

"If you do, Dad will just ply you with more questions about what it's like to live in Beijing," Adam warned.

"We'd love to have you again, if you have time." Her father seemed mollified by Nick's halfhearted promise.

"Did you park your car nearby?" Amber thought back to how she'd found him standing outside their home. She didn't remember seeing any strange cars parked on the road, but she could have missed it. "I'll walk you outside."

Adam raised a brow. "I'll come with you."

Oh please. Like she needed a chaperone for this? "I can handle it." Her narrow glare told him to back off. Her brothers and their protective attitude had worn thin years ago. They always found fault with the guys she dated, except for Shane. And while Shane had kissed her prior to his trip overseas, he hadn't actually asked her out. Not for lack of trying on her part.

Her brothers routinely interfered with other aspects of her life as well. Even when she had gotten her own apartment, Alec, a cop with the Milwaukee Police Department had moved into the same building to keep an eye on her. He claimed the area had a high crime rate. Yeah, right. She'd learned he'd promised her parents he'd look after her. Honestly, she needed to gain independence from her family. Being forced to temporarily move in with her parents had not helped.

"I didn't drive here." Nick's smile seemed strained. "The motel I'm staying at isn't far."

Normally she would have agreed. It was a nice summer night for a walk after all. But she'd noticed the lines bracketing next mouth had grooved deeper as their dinner had worn on. She'd worked with enough patients experiencing pain that she recognized a man in agony when she saw him. She wondered if he'd brought any medications with him, or if he'd left them back at the motel.

He stood and swayed slightly before using one hand to force his knee into a locked position beneath him. Yep. Definitely left his meds at the hotel, she decided. Stubborn man, not to have said anything sooner.

"I'll walk you out," she repeated, ignoring her brothers. For a second she thought Adam was going to follow, but he didn't. Thankfully Alec was working or for sure he would have. Alec saw violent crime everywhere he looked, making him twice as cautious at home. As she strode past the door, she lifted her parents' car keys off the hook mounted on the wall.

She'd sold her car, intent on buying another once she'd settled in Florida. If she needed one. The condo she would be staying in was located close to the hospital, so she doubted she would. Maybe she'd buy a bike instead. Or an electric scooter. Something she could use to ride down to the beach.

Outside, Nick stiffly crossed the porch, then descended the stairs, one painful step at a time.

"Hop in and I'll drive you to the hotel." She gestured to the vehicle parked in the driveway.

"I can walk. Thanks again for dinner." His tone was abrupt, almost rude.

If she hadn't been so accustomed to taking care of people in pain, she might have taken his dismissal personally. However, dealing with her patients and the Dr. Rolands of the world, she'd grown tough.

"Don't be an idiot. Get in the car," she said sharply. "Do you think I can't see how badly you're hurting?"

He paused then turned to look at her as if he couldn't believe her gall. Then understanding dawn. "That's right. I almost forgot you're a nurse."

Her smile was not a bit sweet. "Yes, and if you know what's good for you, you won't argue. Especially now when you look as if one little push would send you sprawling flat on your face. And I have to tell you, there's no way I'll get you up off the street by myself. My brother and sister will have to help."

His jaw tightened and she knew he hated every minute of weakness. But hallelujah, he didn't bite her head off. He turned and hobbled toward the car. "Fine, you can drive me back."

She stood, waiting until he'd slid into the passenger seat, before climbing in on the driver's side. She adjusted the driver's seat forward then backed out of the driveway.

"So, where are you staying?" She kept her tone mild, ignoring the resentment radiating off him in waves.

"A place called The Cozy Inn. It's just six blocks east and one block south of here."

The Cozy Inn? She glanced at him in surprise. "That's right across the street from the VA hospital where I work."

His gaze was enigmatic. "Yeah. Although I didn't know you worked there."

She was dying of curiosity. "What are you doing here in Milwaukee? Other than returning a box of personal mementos, that is."

"Nothing much." He stared out the window as if avoiding her gaze. "I told you, I'm not practicing as a surgeon. I'm still in physical therapy."

"I see." But she really didn't. Drumming her fingers on the steering wheel, she sent him a sidelong glance. Had he come to Milwaukee for a second opinion? She wanted to ask, but that would be rude.

Wouldn't it? Yes. Definitely rude.

"Here we are. The Cozy Inn." She pulled into the motel parking lot. "Where is your room?"

"Ground level, number ten, the room on the end." The motel was small, only two rows of rooms. The upper level sported a covered walkway. In deference to his discomfort, she pulled into the parking slot closest to the doorway near room ten.

She watched as Nick opened the passenger door and tried to swing his legs out of the car. As he struggled, he never uttered a sound, but his forehead was soon covered with a fine sheen of sweat.

Ridiculous. The guy would fall on his backside before requesting a helping hand. With a soundless sigh, she slid out from behind the wheel and stalked around to the passenger side.

"I can't stand it." She glared at him. "It's your left side giving you problems, right?"

Remaining mute, lips compressed in a tight line, he nodded.

"That's what I thought. I'll pull you up then I want you to lean on me." She used both of her hands to clasp his right hand and used her weight to lever him up and off the seat.

He was several shades paler by the time he managed to stand upright. She took a moment to grab his cane, then braced her body under his good arm so that she didn't stress the injured muscles of his left side. Keeping her pace slow, they walked or maybe stumbled, toward the doorway.

He was heavier than he looked, probably because of his height. She wasn't sure how they managed but soon they were standing in front of his motel room door. He had his room key and was swiping it in front of the sensor with his left hand, trying hard not to sway. She imagined anyone walking past them would think Nick was intoxicated or using illegal drugs.

"We're almost there," she said encouragingly as he finally pushed the door open.

Inside, she was glad the room was on the small side as they made their way toward the bed. She was beginning to feel his weight, her own sore muscles protesting the strain.

"Let's turn so you can sit down." She tried to help him pivot, but somehow her legs entwined with his and she felt him tilt sideways.

"No," she cried as she attempted to yank him upright. But it was too late. His heavier weight dragged her down along with him as they bounced on the bed in a helpless tangle of limbs.

CHAPTER THREE

Once the blinding pain receded, Nick wondered if he'd died and gone to heaven. Not because the pain had lessened to a tolerable level but because of Amber's warm vanilla scent filling his head and the softness of her body pressing against his chest. She was sprawled on top of him, her light weight a welcome distraction. He prayed she wouldn't move. Her sweet mouth invited him close.

He didn't know what possessed him to lift the necessary inch to taste her. But once he did, he couldn't make himself regret it. She was sweet, her lips soft. When she didn't pull away or slug him, he gathered her close and took advantage of her startled gasp to deepen the kiss.

How long since he'd held a woman? Or even wanted to? Seemed like a lifetime.

Her eager response as she kissed him back sent warning signals beeping in his brain. He abruptly realized he'd started something he didn't dare finish.

Amber wasn't his to date. She belonged to someone else. Before he could talk himself out of it, he broke off the kiss. Dazed, she stared down at him for a long moment. Then she rolled off him to sit on the edge of the bed. She looked stunned, shaken.

What was wrong with him? He shouldn't have taken advantage of her like this. He'd only been thinking of himself. *Again.*

With a wince, he sat up next to her. As she still hadn't said a word, he felt obligated to apologize. "I'm sorry. I never should have kissed you, especially when you're grieving over losing Shane. I know it's too soon. I didn't intend to take advantage of your kindness. Just chalk this up to a moment of insanity."

Her entire body went still. Then he realized his mistake. Stupid, stupid, stupid! The only reason he knew the extent of her feelings toward Shane was because he'd read her letters and emails.

I miss you, Shane. Things aren't the same around here without you. Especially miss our talks. Have I mentioned what a great listener you are? Even now, writing to you like this isn't the same as two of us laughing and talking for hours. Especially the night right before you left.

He'd become envious of the relationship between Amber and Shane. That's how low he'd sunk, battling a burning resentment toward a dead man.

"What do you know about my feelings for Shane?" Her voice held a deceptive softness, but the glitter in her blue eyes betrayed her true feelings.

He swallowed hard. "Ah—I just figured. I mean, Shane told me how romantically involved the two of you were..."

"Nice try, but I don't believe Shane said anything of the sort." Confusion flickered across her features then her gaze narrowed as realization dawned. "I don't believe it. You read my letters to Shane."

And here it was. He braced himself for the full force of

her anger because he deserved it. "Yes. I didn't mean to, but I did. Read them, I mean. I'm sorry."

"Of all the lowlife stunts." Face flaming, she scrambled to her feet and shot across the motel room to the door. "Those notes were *personal*. You had no right to read them."

"I know." Helpless to do anything else, he watched her storm out of his room, slamming the door behind her for good measure.

He wanted to run after her, to make her understand why he'd read them, but he let her go. For one thing, he couldn't force his aching body to move. And more importantly, she was right. He was very much the lowest form of life on earth. With a heavy sigh, he scrubbed his hands over his face. He couldn't find the words to explain how her letters and notes had changed him. Her positive outlook on life, her self-deprecating humor, and her obvious affection for her family had gotten him through the darkest days of his recovery. Every letter and note had only endeared her to him more. Until he'd yearned to meet her in person.

Now that he had, Amber was even more beautiful than he'd imagined. Their chance meeting in the street outside the Monroe house had caught him off guard. There was no denying the instant flash of awareness, even though she'd looked far too young. He'd been interested in her in a way he hadn't been for a very long time. The way their brief kiss had spun out of control only proved that point.

Too bad, he was the last man on the face of the earth she would ever be interested in.

Even if she was able to get over her anger and embarrassment of how he'd invaded her privacy, there was no use pursuing a relationship. For one thing, he was still a cripple, but worse, she didn't know the truth. If not for Shane's attempts to rescue him, the man she'd deeply cared for would still be alive today.

HOW DARE Nick Tanner read her personal notes to Shane? What right did he have to invade her privacy?

What right did he have to kiss her?

Mortified, she leaned her forehead on the steering wheel and tried to pull herself together. Nick's kiss had thrown her seriously off balance. Then to find out he'd read her personal notes and letters—she swallowed hard. So what if her letters held a friendship tone? They were still personal. She and Shane hadn't even gone on one date, much less anything more serious. If they had been deeply romantically involved, this could have been far worse. A strangled laugh escaped her throat. As if it wasn't bad enough.

Nick probably thought she was hopeless, the way she'd hinted at wanting something more with Shane. She'd chattered about her life, maybe venting a bit over her interfering, overprotective, yet very loving family. Good grief, no wonder Nick had expected someone older. Boring, bitter old maid.

Enough! No use wallowing in self-pity. With sheer grit and determination, she pulled herself together. She would forget about the impact of Nick's potent kiss and his blatant disregard for her privacy. Lifting her head, she started the car. Calmer now, she drove home. It was easy to admit that she was more embarrassed than angry to discover Nick knew all those unflattering things about her.

Not until she'd pulled into her parents' driveway, though, did the question really occur to her.

Why?

Why would Nick Tanner, a trauma surgeon training in Beijing, bother to read notes and letters she'd written to Shane Reinhart?

She stared past the yard rakes and shovels hanging off the back wall of the garage. She had no clue. To be honest, she couldn't comprehend a single, logical reason for Nick to care about what she'd written.

Perturbed, she climbed from the car and headed inside the house. She wasn't in the habit of lying to herself, so she forced herself to examine her true feelings. Was she more embarrassed over her response to Nick's kiss or the way he'd read her letters?

Both. And she couldn't quite pinpoint which of the two events bothered her more.

"MR. GOETZ, it's time for you to go down for physical therapy." Amber stopped the older man in the wheelchair from going in the opposite direction. "That's the way to the dining room. The elevators are down the hall, this way." She turned his chair back around.

"I'm not going to therapy." He glared at her, then with surprising strength spun himself so he was headed to the dining room again. "I'm too tired for therapy."

She suppressed her sigh. She understood how difficult it was for these patients to force themselves to face the pain of physical therapy, yet at the same time they'd never get any better if they didn't work their injured muscles. The image of Nick flashed in her mind's eye. He likely spent hours in physical therapy, too. She wondered again why he'd come to

Milwaukee. To see a specialist? Or was he still under a doctor's care at home?

Where did Nick call home?

"Mr. Goetz, you know the rules," she explained again. A big part of being accepted to the rehabilitation floor meant tolerating three hours of therapy per day. He might be one of her favorite patients, but this was for his own good. "You must attend therapy, even if only for a short while. Unless you're sick in bed, which you obviously aren't."

For a moment the stubborn old man glared at her, then his shoulders slumped. "I'm just too tired."

Her heart squeezed in sympathy, but she steeled her resolve. "I know. But you need to at least give it a try. Please? Once you're in the gym, working your muscles I'm sure you'll feel less tired. And if not, tell the therapist to call me and I'll run down and get you."

He blew out a deep, heavy sigh. "All right." He allowed her to turn his chair around and wheel him down the hall toward the elevators. She had a million other things to do, but wheeled Mr. Goetz into the elevator and rode down with him.

When the doors opened, she pushed his chair down the hall and into the spacious gym area. Equipment of all kinds lined the walls, including some exercise machines. Wide exercise mats were scattered around the center of the room for muscle strengthening activities. A set of parallel bars for independent standing and walking stood on the opposite side of the room. For a second, a man with his back to her using the bars reminded her of Nick. Then she laughed at her own foolishness. She was imagining him everywhere. The guy haunted her because of one simple, silly kiss.

Paul, one of the physical therapists on duty, crossed the

room and greeted his patient. "Good morning, Mr. Goetz. How are you feeling today?"

She hadn't seen Paul since the last time he'd asked her out, but forced a smile and gave her head a slight shake. "Mr. Goetz isn't feeling very energetic today. Maybe you can start him off slow, hmm?"

Paul Fletcher sent her a questioning glance, but nodded. "Sure thing. We'll work on the floor mat first—how about that?"

"I guess so." Mr. Goetz was less than enthused.

"Thanks." She reached down to gently squeeze Mr. Goetz's arm. "Take care. I'll see you upstairs in a little while."

"Yeah, yeah," he groused.

Paul wheeled Mr. Goetz toward the mat and she stared after them for a minute. Paul was a nice guy, but she couldn't summon any interest in him, there was no spark of attraction at all. At the time, she'd wondered if she'd ever get over losing Shane.

Until she'd met Nick.

Her cheeks flushed as she remembered those brief moments he'd held her in his arms. Apparently, she wasn't immune to a good looking guy after all. It hadn't taken much for her to have come alive in Nick's embrace. The man could kiss. Never had her heart gone from zero to ninety like that, leaving her wanting more.

As much as it pained her to admit it, Shane's kiss hadn't roused such an instantaneous response.

Thank goodness Nick had broken off the kiss before she'd made a complete fool of herself.

She swallowed hard and turned away. One kiss didn't mean she was interested in anything more. She couldn't wait to get out of the city and to start living her life. A relationship would interfere with her desire to travel. Besides, Nick wasn't her type. She preferred friendly, outgoing guys like Shane. They'd taken long walks and spent hours talking. Shane's personality suited her far better. Tall, dark and brooding didn't appeal to her.

Too bad, because Nick was devastatingly attractive.

Shaking off the useless thoughts, she decided to take the stairs up to the second floor rehab unit. She'd reached the top landing when the overhead speaker came on.

"Medical emergency, first floor, physical therapy gym. Medical emergency, first floor, physical therapy gym."

Mr. Goetz. Instinctively, she knew her patient was in trouble. Although she wasn't a part of the medical emergency response team, she turned and raced back down the stairs to the first floor.

She burst into the gym area and saw a group of people crowded around the physical therapy floor mat. She pushed her way into the center. "What happened?"

"He's having a seizure." Nick glanced up at her from where he sat beside Mr. Goetz. "Does he take medication for seizures?

She couldn't believe Nick was there, dressed in light gray sweats, and realized her mind hadn't been playing tricks on her after all. She forced herself to quickly review Mr. Goetz's medical history. "No, he doesn't. He's never had a seizure before that I'm aware of."

"Good to know." Nick's attention was focused on the patient. "Where's the code cart? I want the intubation equipment ready once the seizure has passed."

"I have it right here." Paul opened the bottom drawer of the yellow cart next to him and pulled out a smaller bin holding various airway equipment. He quickly positioned it beside Nick.

"Maybe we should intubate him now?" She placed a hand a Mr. Goetz's arm, feeling each tremor down to the soles of her feet. "He's not breathing very well."

"I can't intubate him until the seizure is over. His jaw muscles are locked tight."

She sensed Nick's frustration. As they both stared at Mr. Goetz, his face grew dusky. She found herself holding her own breath as she watched. Would his heart handle the strain?

"The medical response team should be here at any minute," Paul informed them.

Amber knew the physical therapy gym was located on the opposite side of the building from where the intensive care units were located. And it was those staff members who took turns responding to medical emergencies.

The movement beneath her hands stopped. She glanced up at Nick. "The seizure is over."

"I'm going to intubate him. He's already post-ictal." Nick reached for the equipment he'd already set up. "Amber, hold him steady."

Did Nick have medical practice privileges here? She wasn't sure, but breaking policy was a minor concern compared to the threat of losing Mr. Goetz.

"What else can I do?" She didn't have critical care experience, but understood the basics. This was required training for all staff members in the VA hospital.

"Connect the heart monitor while I give him some breaths with the Ambu bag." Nick had already hooked up the Ambu bag to the portable oxygen tank on the cart.

"All right." Her fingers fumbled with the unfamiliar task, but soon had the electrodes placed and her elderly patient's chest. The beeping of Mr. Goetz's heart on the monitor was reassuring.

Nick gave him one last breath then set the Ambu bag aside and reached for the laryngoscope. Amber held on to Mr. Goetz while Nick opened the elderly man's mouth and peered into the back of his throat to visualize the trachea. With a deft movement he slid the breathing tube into place.

The beeping and the heart monitor slowed down.

She gasped. "I think his heart rhythm is changing."

At that moment, the rest of the medical emergency team arrived.

"Do you need help?" The resident physician spoke between panting breaths from his mad dash from the ICU.

"Yes, he needs an IV so we can give him a milligram of atropine." Nick finished securing the endotracheal tube, then pulled the stylet out. "Amber, hand me the Easycap so we can check the tube placement."

"Okay." When placed on the end of the endotracheal tube, the Easycap device changed color if correctly placed in the patient's airway and not his esophagus, the tube leading to his stomach. She slid the device on the end of the tube. Relief washed over her when the yellow color confirmed the breathing tube was correctly placed.

"Placement is good." She took the device off then connected the Ambu bag to the endotracheal tube. "Listen for breath sounds."

"I need a stethoscope."

The resident who'd run to their emergency handed his over.

Nick listened as she gave big breaths with the Ambu bag. She watched the monitor. Mr. Goetz's heartbeat improved with the delivery of oxygen. "I hear breath sounds on both sides. And his pulse is stable. Let's hold off on the atropine," Nick said.

"He needs to be transferred to the ICU." The resident took over the situation. "What happened?"

"A seizure, although he doesn't have a history of them." A detail that continued to nag at her. What could possibly have caused Mr. Goetz to have a seizure? "He's in rehab because of a broken left hip. He was due to go to a nursing home in a few days, but he's on a waiting list. I can get the rest of his stuff out of his room and bring it up to the ICU."

"Sounds good." More staff members arrived with a gurney. Together, the team transferred Mr. Goetz from the gym mat up and onto the cart.

She stood back, allowing the medical emergency team to take her patient away. She glanced at Nick, who used a cane to help him stand. "I am surprised to see you here, but am very thankful that you were around to help."

He shrugged. "I'm still getting therapy three times a week. I've been employed by the government for years, which gives me certain privileges to be treated at any VA hospital."

"I see." His choice of staying at The Cozy Inn, located directly across from the hospital, wasn't accidental. "Does that mean you have practice privileges here?"

He looked thoughtful. "Technically, yes. I'm on medical leave as far as being a surgeon goes, but I still have a license to practice medicine." He glanced around. "I hope the upper brass doesn't hold my responding to the medical emergency against me."

"Mr. Goetz didn't want to go to therapy this morning." She blurted out her deepest concern. "I made him come down. When I heard the medical emergency being called. I knew it was him."

He placed a comforting hand on her arm. "It's not your fault. If he had a seizure, there's a medical reason for it."

"I know." She thought back over Mr. Goetz's rehab stay. "His biggest complaint recently has been stubborn urinary tract infections. And I think there were a couple of days he complained of a headache." A wave of doubt swelled, stealing the breath from her lungs. Had she missed something important?

"Did the rehab doc work up his infections and his headache?"

"We gave him Tylenol and double strength Bactrim." She scowled. "Dr. Roland doesn't make rounds very often."

Nicks gaze sharpened. "What do you mean?"

She bit her lip, hesitated, then spread her hands. She'd started this, she may as well finish it. "Just what I said. Dr. Roland doesn't make rounds very often. In fact, if we didn't call him with issues, we wouldn't even know he was the physician of record."

CHAPTER FOUR

After Amber returned to her nursing unit, Nick returned to his therapy. Sweat rolled off his forehead, burning his eyes as he worked his injured leg on the exercise equipment. He tried to wipe his brow on the short sleeve of his T-shirt without losing his grip. He grasped the dual hand rests, using every bit of strength he had to lever the weights upward. They were only set at a measly twenty pounds but each repetition felt like some masochist had moved the pin to the one hundred pound mark.

Blazing pain radiating through his body reminded him of the plane crash, when he'd spent countless hours wedged in the wrecked plane, struggling to crawl out despite his broken pelvis, multiple compound fractures of his left leg and left dislocated shoulder. He hadn't even realized until later about his fractured fingers.

Working the painful muscles now, he knew he was lucky to be alive. A life he owed to Shane Reinhart. Most of the time he'd spent in the hospital was a dark blur. After his initial emergency surgery in China, he'd been transferred back to the United States, courtesy of the US government.

There were times it was nice to be employed by Uncle Sam. That's when he'd received his box of personal belongings from Beijing, only to find his stuff commingled with Shane's.

After finishing the thirty painful reps, he dropped the weights with a clatter then sat back with a sigh.

He was thankful to be alive. No question about that. For a moment he stared at his left hand, specifically the three fingers numb from nerve damage from his dislocated shoulder and broken fingers. What was he going to do if the damaged muscles didn't heal well enough for him to return to the operating room? He was right-handed, but no surgeon operated with only one hand. His goal through medical school had been to become a trauma surgeon. Yes, there were plenty of other specialties out there, but he hadn't considered anything else. Now, that was all he could think about. He closed the injured fingers into a fist. His hand might be getting better, he'd managed to intubate Amber's patient, but the simple procedure didn't take as much finesse as performing intricate surgery did.

As usual, he didn't want to dwell on his bleak thoughts.

Amber's blunt summation of the rehab doctor's practice flashed through his mind. His specialty wasn't physical medicine, but he knew very well that the standard of care for rehab wasn't much different from any other medical service. Physicians were expected to see their patients in the hospital on a regular basis.

If Amber was correct, Roland wasn't even meeting the minimum requirement dictated by their profession.

Nick stood and slowly, gingerly, used his cane to make his way across the physical therapy gym. Pretty sad when his toughest decision of the day was whether or not he should shower here or return to his motel room across the street. With a snort, he turned toward the main doors. He'd choose the privacy of his motel room.

"Are you all finished, Dr. Tanner?" The physical therapist, Paul, stopped him before he reached the doorway.

"Yes, for now. I'll probably be back tomorrow, though."

"No problem. I'll be here," Paul assured him.

Nick was about to leave, then he turned back. "There's a doctor here by the name of Roland who works on the rehab unit."

Paul raised his eyebrows. "You mean the medical director of rehabilitation services?"

Medical director? How could a guy who didn't make routine rounds be the medical director of the unit? Nick swallowed his surprise. Had Amber exaggerated Roland's lax attitude? From what little he knew about her, she didn't seem the type to overstate the truth.

"Yeah, I guess that's the guy. What's his first name?"

"Douglas." If Paul was curious about his line of questioning, the therapist didn't show it. Probably figured with his messed up body, Nick was asking for personal reasons, like seeking a new doctor.

If what Amber said was true, Roland would be the last on his list if he did need a referral.

"Douglas Roland," he repeated. The name wasn't familiar, but he committed it to memory. There were dozens of VA hospitals across the nation. There was no reason for him to know this particular doc, although he had worked in several of them. "Thanks." He'd use the hospital computer system, another government perk, to check Roland out and see what information he could find.

Anything was better than sitting around, feeling useless.

HOURS LATER NICK didn't have any concrete answers. After a shower and a change of clothes, he'd made himself at home in the hospital library, using the computer to find out what he could about standards of practice regarding physician rounds. The only thing he'd learned for certain was that a rehab was a step down from acute care, and as such, the physician was only expected to make rounds every two days, whereas daily rounds were required for inpatient physicians.

Amber had a right to be concerned about the care her patients received, though. He wished there was something more he could do to help.

He did another search and found Roland's boss, the chief of staff, listed as a Dr. Rick Johnson. There was also an opening for a temporary hospitalist in the department of physical medicine. He stared at the job posting for a long time. Interesting. Maybe he could fill in for a while, to give him something constructive to do. And perhaps help Amber at the same time. Of course, he'd have to run this idea past his boss back in Virginia first. Somehow he didn't think Steven White would mind. Before he could chicken out and change his mind, he placed a call to his boss. Steven wasn't in so he left a brief message.

Turning his attention back to the computer he did another search under Dr. Douglas Roland all he found out was that the guy had apparently been at the hospital here in Milwaukee for the past six years, the last two as the medical director. How had the guy managed to get promoted was a mystery. Unless he'd only started to slack off once he'd obtained the medical director role.

Glancing at his watch, he was surprised to note the hour was already past noon. Amber's shift probably ended at 3:00 if they were doing eight-hour shifts, rather than twelve.

There had been a mishmash of schedules back in Virginia, so he couldn't be sure. He'd grab something to eat in the hospital cafeteria, then wander up to the rehab unit to find her.

Anticipation tightened in his belly even though he knew better than to think of Amber on a personal level. She was far too good for him. He was impressed with her skills as a nurse. That morning she'd been all business, her grave expression betraying her genuine concern for her patient. He'd gathered from her letters how seriously she took her responsibilities, which was the main reason he'd expected someone older.

One of my patients died three days after we discharged home. He took his own life, Shane. I can't stop thinking about it. I should have looked harder to find a hint of his depression. I even went back into the system to review all the nursing notes, but I wasn't the only one who missed it. We all did. Or maybe we simply didn't want to see how depressed he was, I don't know. There is no way to go back and fix things now, but this young man's death weighs heavily on my conscience. I pray for him and others who may be suffering the same illness, every night.

For some reason her brief story stayed with him. Maybe because he could relate to the depression that kid must have felt. With the help of Amber's letter, he had been able to recognize his own feelings and fight off the black cloud when it loomed too close.

He was secretly relieved she didn't have any clue how much he'd hung on her every word.

The cafeteria was crowded. He tried to skirt around a group of medical students, and nearly dropped his tray on the floor when he tried to balance the thing with one hand while leaning on his cane with the other. He managed to set the tray down on the nearest vacant table, but his chest burned with pent up frustration. He was barely self-sufficient. How much longer would he have to limp around before he'd be back to his normal self?

Maybe forever.

Bile rose into his throat and he forced it back with several deep breaths. No, he refused to believe the worst. He was truly thankful for his life, but was it so wrong to want his old career back?

Ignoring the hospital employees seated at various tables around him, he concentrated on swallowing each bite of his food without tasting a thing. Protein equaled strength, and strength would lead to building and repairing his torn and injured muscle mass. He didn't dare miss a meal, no matter how much he didn't feel like eating. He pushed away the haunting thoughts about his career, or lack thereof, and focused on what he needed to do to get through the day.

The hour was close to three when he finally made his way upstairs. He stopped at the information desk in the lobby to find out where the rehab unit was located. He assumed it wouldn't be too far from the physical therapy gym and discovered the unit was located just one floor above it.

He didn't see Amber in the hallway, but the familiar clinical scent stopped him cold. Ugh, how could he have forgotten? Hospitals always carried the strong scent of antiseptic, but this was different. The scent of urine was stronger here, probably because many of the patients were unable to take care of their most basic needs.

His fingers tightened on the head of his cane. A few short weeks ago, he'd been one of them. The smell brought back a flood of memories, none of them good. Forcing himself to move, he walked slowly down the long hall toward the nurse's station. He noticed a few patients, mostly men, sitting in wheelchairs in the hallways, or in the doorways to their rooms. But he didn't see anyone from the nursing staff.

Then he understood why. Change of shift meant nurses were giving report to each other, as they transferred care from one shift to the next. He stood awkwardly, feeling stupid and trying not to dwell on the horrible memories of being a patient himself.

All his instincts shouted at him to leave, to get out of there before someone realized they'd made a mistake by discharging him too soon and tossed him back into a hospital bed.

He licked his dry lips and tried to remind himself he was a doctor, not a patient. He'd have to get used to being in the hospital environment again. Difficult to be a physician if he wasn't working in a hospital setting. He needed to put those painful memories of being a patient aside once and for all. Better to start now in a different rehab unit than the one he'd spent time in.

Despite his internal pep talk, standing amidst the rehab patients was far from easy.

AMBER FINISHED GIVING REPORT, then walked out to the front of the desk. Now that her eight-hour shift was over, she wanted to head over to the ICU to check on Mr. Goetz. During her lunch break, she'd gone to see him but he'd been down in radiology, having an MRI scan of his head. All day, she'd wondered how he was doing.

"Hi, Amber."

Surprised, she glanced over to see Nick standing on the

opposite side of the nurse's station. Her pulse kicked up a notch when she saw him. He'd showered, shaved and changed from the gray sweat pants and T-shirt into khaki pants and a dark blue polo shirt. It seemed wrong that he had the power to take her breath away. No matter what he wore. She tried to sound casual. "Hey, Nick. What are you doing up here?"

"Just being nosy, I guess. Do you have a minute to show me around the unit?" Nick held her gaze with his.

Part of her wanted to refuse. She needed, for the sake of her sanity, to check on Mr. Goetz. But if there was a chance Nick could help her get someone's attention about Dr. Roland, she decided she'd better take it.

"Sure. Just give me a minute to grab my purse." She turned back to the report room to fetch her purse from her locker. Then she rounded the desk and approached him. As he had that first night, he stood painfully straight, holding onto his cane. Up close, the tangy sent of his aftershave teased her senses. She almost leaned forward to inhale more deeply, then caught herself. What was wrong with her? She cleared her throat. "We have a thirty bed rehab unit." She gestured to one hallway. "The brain injury patients are normally housed in the center wing, the musculoskeletal injuries are on the right."

Nick frowned. "What happens if one of the head injury patients wanders off?"

"We have alarms that sound if a patient leaves the unit unattended," she assured him. "We use a wander guard type of system. Trust me the alarm is loud. Every staff member would be alerted if someone left the unit."

Seemingly impressed, he nodded. "Good."

"The dining room is at the end of this hall." She headed down that way, although there weren't too many patients seated in the dining room area at this hour. "We think it's good for our patients to get out of their rooms to eat in a common place.

"Hmm." Nick's shrug was noncommittal, and she wondered what he thought of the practice when he'd been a patient. No doubt he'd been as grumpy as Mr. Goetz. His familiarity with rehab was obvious. She imagined patience wasn't his strong suit.

"This is a nice area, but I noticed the third wing is completely empty. Why haven't you moved the physical therapy gym to this floor? Wouldn't that be more convenient for your patients?"

"Yes, it would." She sighed. "We suggested that very thing two years ago, but the planned renovation didn't survive budget cuts." It still burned to know Roland's new office had been completed, featuring cherry wood furniture and floor to ceiling bookcases, but not the relocation of the gym. She didn't want to keep bashing Dr. Roland but, honestly, with him in charge, it seemed nothing happened to facilitate better patient care.

"Roland isn't around, I take it?" It seemed as if he'd read her uncharitable thoughts.

"No, he's not." She turned back leading the way toward the main nurse's station. Talking about Roland would only make her mad.

"Is your shift over?" Nick asked as they walked off the rehab unit.

She thought about how he must feel being in a strange city all alone. Despite her annoyance with the way he'd read her letters, she couldn't manage to stay angry with him. The idea of Nick sitting in his tiny motel room for the rest of the evening bothered her.

"Yes, I'm off, thank goodness." She flashed a quick smile.

"You know, my dad would be thrilled if you'd come over for dinner again. I know you're probably sick of his incessant questions, but if you're not too busy, we'd love to have you."

He shook his head with a wry smile. "I know your parents were close to Shane, but he wasn't their son. I'm not sure I understand why your dad is so interested."

Amber suspected she'd gotten her longing for adventure from her dad. He'd always wanted to travel too, but there wasn't much sightseeing you could do with six kids whose ages spanned 11 years. She didn't want to go into all that detail though so she gave him the shortened version.

"Shane was around all the time when he and Adam were younger. Then his parents moved out of state while he and Adam were still in high school. Shane moved in for the last two years of high school, until he and Adam graduated. Then he and Adam both went to college in Madison majoring in pre med."

Nick arched a brow. "I didn't realize your brother was a physician, too."

"Yes, but he specializes in pediatrics." She glanced at her watch then gestured to the elevator. "What do you think? Will you come for dinner?

A shadow passed over his eyes, then quickly disappeared. "Sure. Why not?"

"Great. We can go after I make a quick stop in the ICU."

"To see Mr. Goetz?" Nick guessed.

"Yep."

They rode the elevator to the 4th floor. The ICU was on the other side of the building, so she headed down the hall, slowing her pace to accommodate his lopsided gait.

"I tried to see Mr. Goetz earlier but he was having an MRI scan. I hope he's doing alright."

"I'm curious to see how he's faring, too."

"What do you think caused his seizure?"

"Hard to say." Nick shrugged. "Could be anything from a brain tumor to a blood clot. You mentioned urinary tract infections, he could have thrown a clot from being septic. Whatever the source, his MRI will tell them what they need to know."

She fell silent as they approached the ICU. She'd never worked there, and she found the environment intimidating. He didn't seem to notice her apprehension, while she used her hospital ID badge to scan the sensor that opened the automatic doors. She could just imagine what an imposing picture he would make as the trauma surgeon in charge.

The unit clerk raised her head as they entered. "Hello, may I help you?"

She stepped forward with determination. "Yes, we'd like to see Mr. Goetz, if you don't mind. I'm his nurse from the rehab unit. And this is Dr. Nick Tanner. He helped with the medical resuscitation."

"Oh, uh, Okay. Just a minute. "The clerk appeared flustered as she reached for the phone. "Mary? The floor nurse is here to see your patient in bed twelve."

"Something's wrong," Nick murmured beside her. "His name isn't on the board."

What board? Leaning forward, she saw it. The main census board for the unit was tucked around the corner out of view. As her gaze traveled down the list of names, the warning knot in her stomach tightened like a noose.

An older nurse, wearing scrubs, came over to them. "Hi, my name is Mary. I understand you're here to see Mr. Goetz."

"Yes. I was his nurse on the rehab floor and witnessed

his seizure. Is he okay? Did you transfer him to the general floor already?"

Mary's gaze turned sympathetic. "No, I'm sad to say Mr. Goetz died about an hour ago."

She reached for Nick and his hand closed around hers with reassuring strength as the nurse continued.

"We did the MRI and found a large brain tumor. They wanted to take him to the OR but he suffered a cardiac arrest before they could get him there. Considering his prognosis, his new tumor combined with the infection in his blood stream, there wasn't anything more we could do." Mary shrugged helplessly. "I'm sorry."

Me, too, Amber thought, overwhelmed with sadness. *Me, too.*

CHAPTER FIVE

For a horrible moment Nick feared Amber might faint. A determined expression flittered across her face, making him realize he should have known better. She was made of sterner stuff than that. Her hand clutched his as if it were a lifeline, but she remained calm. His admiration for her rose another notch.

"Thanks for letting us know." Her voice held a slight tremor.

"You're welcome. I just wish we had better news." With an apologetic smile, the ICU nurse hurried off.

"Come on, we need to get out of here." Nick tried to edge her toward the door, wishing there was something he could do to ease her pain.

"I made him go to therapy. He said he was too tired and I made him go, anyway." she whispered. "What kind of nurse am I?"

He was all too familiar with the confusion laced with guilt likely ricocheting through her head. Hadn't he been there himself four months ago? Guilt was a powerful emotion.

"A great nurse." He spoke firmly. "There is no way you could have known he had a brain tumor. He could have just as easily had a seizure during breakfast as during physical therapy."

"Logically I know you're right." Her tone lacked conviction. "I just wish I wouldn't have made him go."

Somehow, he managed to get her out of the ICU and down the hall to the waiting room. There, he stopped and pulled her close with his good arm. "I'm really sorry that you're going through this."

She leaned into his embrace. Her warm vanilla scent helped him ignore the flash of pain from the added stress on his injured leg. "It's okay. I'll be fine."

He shouldn't have been so keenly aware of the softness of her body pressed against his. Despite the pain along his left side, he wanted to draw her closer still, hugging her close. Their brief embrace ended far too quickly, as she pulled away a few moments later.

"Let's get out of here." Her voice was stronger now.

"Only if you're really okay." He didn't mind giving her the time she needed to grieve for her patient.

"I'll be fine," she repeated. "I did tell Roland about his headaches, though. And I wish I had pressed harder for Roland to pay attention to his symptoms."

He hesitated, feeling compelled to point out the truth. "Even if Roland had made rounds and had known about Mr. Goetz's recent headaches, chances are he wouldn't have ordered any additional treatment. Brain tumors are extremely hard to diagnose without more severe symptoms. It's not like every person with a headache gets an MRI scan of their brain."

She let out a heavy sigh. "I know." She tapped her temple. "You know how nurses have gallows humor. We all make jokes about it, saying stuff like, 'I have a headache. Hope it's not a brain tumor.' But I still worry Mr. Goetz might have had other symptoms we missed. Symptoms a better doctor than Roland may have picked up on."

"Maybe, but maybe not." He longed to reach for her again, but forced himself to keep his hands at his sides. "Don't dwell on this. You did the best you could with the information you had."

"I'll try not to." She drew in a deep ragged breath and offered a lopsided smile, although her blue eyes were still suspiciously bright.

"Good. Ready to go?" When she nodded, he steered her toward the elevators with a gentle hand on the small of her back while leaning on his cane with the other. The heat of her skin beneath the thin scrubs, seemed to sear the tips of his fingers. Why was he suddenly so keenly aware of this woman? Any woman, really. But especially Amber, who deserved someone better than him. For years he'd been focused on his career, then after the accident, on getting back on his feet. This hyper awareness for her didn't factor into his plans. He tried to think of something to distract from his tumultuous thoughts. "Do you want to walk the couple of blocks to your parents' house?"

"Sure."

They took the elevator down to the first floor lobby, but once outside Amber abruptly halted mid-stride.

"Wait a minute. I'd rather stop at your motel room first."

He nearly tripped over his cane, his heart hammering in his chest. What did she mean by that? He stared at her in shock and had to remind himself to breathe. "You do? Why?"

"Yes." She sent him an impatient glance. "We are not walking all the way to my parents without getting your pain medication first. Last night you were in so much pain, you could barely make it home, remember?"

"Oh. Yeah." He pulled himself together for an effort. Of course she wasn't interested in kissing him again. It was nice that she cared about making sure he wasn't in pain. "Okay." He cleared his throat and glanced across the street to where his motel was located. "You can wait here if you like. I won't be long."

"I'd rather walk with you." She fell into step beside him. After a few minutes, she lifted her face toward the sky and closed her eyes. "The sun feels so good."

He glanced away, tempted beyond belief to kiss her again. He had to stop thinking about her as an attractive woman. Especially one who would not appreciate his culpability in Shane's death. He cleared his throat and focused on the weather. "Yes, it does. Summertime in Wisconsin is pretty nice."

"Where did you grow up?" She glanced at him as they waited for a break in traffic before crossing the street.

"Chicago." He didn't like talking about his past, it was a good way to ruin a cheerful mood. "Chicago isn't all that far from Milwaukee. We were practically neighbors."

She chuckled. Before he could ask anything further though he forestalled her by asking a few questions of his own.

"What happened to your mother? I think it's great the way you and your siblings have pulled together to help her."

"She got tangled with Murphy, took a header down the stairs and broke her hip. Because of our medical background, Adam and I have taken on most of our mom's personal cares, including going to all her doctor's appointments. Andrea has taken over the household chores with some help from Alec when he's not arresting bad guys. He's a cop." She frowned. "Dad tries to help with Mom, but he isn't as young as he used to be either."

He unlocked the door to his hotel room and pushed it open. Being here with her made him remember the kiss they'd shared the night before. Had it really only been less than twenty-four hours ago? It didn't seem possible.

"I'll be right back." He ducked into the small bathroom.

The pill bottles lined up along the edge of the sink gave him pause. He shook his head. Amber's mother probably didn't have as many prescriptions as he did. Resentment flared, hot and slick. He was tempted to swipe the whole bunch into the toilet and flushed them away.

Only the memory of how hard it had been to use the weight machine earlier stopped him. As much as he detested his physical limitations, he wasn't so sure he'd be able to get himself out of bed in the morning without the stupid pills.

He was weaning himself off them, slowly but surely. He was down to three times a day and, hopefully, soon he'd only need them in the morning and then again at night. And in some ways, the pain helped remind him he was still alive.

He opened his closed his hand again trying to fight off a sense of panic. He refused to think the worst. His hand and his leg were getting better every day.

Maybe.

Muttering under his breath, he grabbed his pain meds off the bathroom sink, stuffed a few in his pocket, then slammed the bottle back down before going out to find Amber.

She turned from the window when he crossed the threshold into the main room. Some of his self-loathing evaporated when he was struck by how the sun brightened her hair, like a halo.

Time to get out of this motel room. He was beginning to wax poetic which was so unlike him. This woman was messing with his brain. As if his body wasn't messed up enough.

He crossed the room and opened the door. "Ready?"

She nodded and stepped up to precede him outside. He closed the hotel door and they started down the street. They hadn't walked very far when the sound of music filled the air.

"Listen!" She grabbed his hand, her eyes bright with excitement. "Do you hear that? There's a park just one block over. Come on, I bet there's a band playing there." She reached for his hand to tug him toward the intersection, intent on changing their course, but then just as abruptly stopped. "Oh, I'm sorry. I forgot about your leg. We don't need to go."

"I'm fine." He was irritated by her hesitation but knew she couldn't help her nursing instincts. He managed a smile. "Walking is good for me. And listening to music is a nice way to relax after a long day."

"Yes, exactly." A shadow fell over her gaze and he knew she was thinking about Mr. Goetz. "Are you sure?" When he nodded, she smiled and turned toward the intersection.

"You must be a fan of jazz." He stood beside her, waiting for the light to change.

Her lips curved in a lopsided smile. "Yes. Jazz was also one of Shane's favorites."

The kernel of guilt returned, nagging like a sore tooth. Should he tell her what had happened? No matter how much she deserved the truth, he didn't know if he could bear seeing the innocent expression on her face turned to one of sheer disgust after she learned exactly how Shane had died.

Especially when he should have been the one to die instead.

No one would have mourned his loss if he had left this earth, except maybe his boss. No family, no girlfriend, no kids. He had spent his life doing whatever he liked without ties to anyone.

Self-centered? You bet. Self-centered was his middle name.

As the approached the park, he noted there was a crowd of people, some standing others sitting on the grass around the spot where a four-piece jazz band belted out some good old fashioned blues.

The neighborhood gathering was very different from what he'd grown up with in Chicago. Milwaukee was smaller than Chicago, but still bigger than most. Yet this park atmosphere seemed more like something you'd find in a small town.

Amber tapped her foot in time to the music and he imagined she loved to dance. He set his jaw. His leg didn't hold up to walking, much less dancing. No matter how determined he was to comply with his therapy, he often wondered if he'd ever get back to normal.

His cell phone rang. Glancing at the screen, he recognized his boss's number. Plugging one ear with his fingertips so he could hear better, he answered, "This is Tanner."

"Got your message." Steven white's booming voice was easy to hear, especially since the band had chosen that moment to take a break. "I think it's a great idea for you to try out the temporary hospitalist position. I might be able to create a full-time position here in Virginia if you decide to go that route, but I'll have to move some budget money around, first."

"I don't know about that." The idea of doing this type of work on a permanent basis didn't sit well with him. He wasn't ready to give up being a surgeon. A temporary position was just that, temporary.

"Your decision," Steven agreed. "See how it goes. I'll get in touch with the chief of staff, Rick Johnson. I'll happily give you a recommendation if you need one."

"Thanks. I'll find Johnson first thing in the morning," he promised.

"Good. Glad to hear it. How are you doing, otherwise?" Steven asked. He knew his boss's question was aimed at getting information about him on a personal level. Specifically, his physical therapy.

"Excellent," he lied. He had no intention of whining to his boss and mentor about his physical problems. From the way Steven had offered to create a different role for him, he figured his boss wasn't confident he'd make it back to the operating room either. Regardless of how he was or wasn't doing. "I'm sorry, but I have to go. I'll let you know what happens after I talk to Johnson."

"Okay. Take care."

Nick ended the call and lowered his phone, feeling a surge of anticipation he hadn't experienced in a long time. Tomorrow he'd talk to Johnson about the position. One he'd normally be over-qualified for. Pathetic to be so excited about a temporary hospitalist role. But he might be able to do good in more ways than one. Like helping Amber. If the rehab unit's medical director really wasn't doing his job, then he would be in a position to do something about it.

Her eyes were bright with curiosity. "What was all that about? Johnson? As in the chief of staff—that Dr. Johnson?"

He slowly nodded. The crowd around them had thinned with the band's break, so they continued to walk toward her parent's house. "Yes, there is a temporary hospitalist position open on the rehab unit. I thought maybe I could fill the role for a little while and see how things are running up there. My boss back in Virginia, gave me the go ahead to discuss the position with Johnson."

"Really?" Her expression turned hopeful.

He grimaced. "It's not exactly as if I'm overwhelmingly busy at the moment."

"I'm so glad." Relief relaxed her tense features. "After the way Roland spoke to me the other day, I can't wait to see how he behaves with a new physician around."

He frowned. "What did he say to you?"

"It doesn't matter." She waved him off with an impatient gesture. "I was rude first. It got me a note in my file and a mandatory training session, but it was worth it."

"Wait a minute. Your personnel file? What on earth happened?"

Now her cheeks were tinged pink. "Nothing. I told you, I was rude first."

This time, it was her cell phone that rang. Irritated she lifted the device to her ear. "I'm on my way, Andrea. Tell Mom not to worry."

When she'd finished her call, he glanced at her. "I'm going to keep bugging you until you tell me what happened."

She rolled her eyes. "Alright, if you must know, I paged him several times about Mr. Goetz."

"And?" He prompted when she paused.

"And, when he finally called back four hours later, he acted as if I paged him for nothing."

From what he knew of Amber, he couldn't imagine she'd paged the guy for nothing. "Jerk."

"Exactly." She grinned. "So I point blank asked if he'd bother responding to his page next time. He got pretty angry, and yelled at me for insinuating he did not take good care of his patients. Which wasn't wrong. That's exactly what I intended."

He chuckled. "Good for you."

"Yeah well, the nurse working with me was horrified. And my nursing director wasn't too thrilled with me, either. Most of the nurses I work with are either brand new and too afraid to speak up or they've been there forever and don't want to make any waves. I don't get it. It's the patients who are suffering."

She turned and led the way up the sidewalk to her parents' front porch. Nick heard her father call out before they even reached the door.

"Amber? Is that you?"

"Yes, Dad. And guess what? I convinced Nick to come for dinner again." She sent him a teasing smile that kicked his pulse into triple digits.

"Great. Bring him in, then. Nick, what can I get you to drink?" Abe greeted him as if he didn't already have four sons of his own. "Lemonade? Iced tea? Soft drink?"

"Whatever you're having is fine." He stood in the living room across from the massive wall of pictures and wondered if this sensation of coming home was how Shane had felt. For a moment he stood still, as if paralyzed.

Shane had saved his life, and now he was here, stealing Shane's place the adopted son of the Monroe household. Worse, he wanted Shane's woman, too.

Could he possibly sink any lower?

AMBER RACED upstairs to find her mother had already gotten herself washed and dressed, and was working on combing her wet hair.

Guilt washed over her. "Mom, I'm so sorry I'm late. Why didn't you wait for me?"

"You were the one telling me I needed to start doing things for myself," Alice reminded her. "You can't get mad when I take your advice."

"I am not mad, just worried." She eased the brush from her mom's hand then went to work on the tangles. "So how did it go? You didn't slip or anything, did you?"

"I didn't take a bath, just sat in a chair and showered," her mother admitted. "Getting in and out was hard enough, even with the help of a chair."

She momentarily closed her eyes. She was so glad her mother hadn't fallen. Instead of coming straight home after work, she dawdled with Nick. Had taken time to enjoy a few minutes of the jazz in the park festival. And maybe, she'd even secretly hoped for a repeat performance of his toe curling kiss.

She really had to stop daydreaming about the man. For one thing, he wasn't interested in her. Hadn't he been the one who had pulled away after their one and only kiss? Yes. Besides, she didn't like the way her mind constantly compared him to Shane, especially when Shane was the one who came up lacking.

Comparing them was ridiculous and grossly unfair. Shane had been a great friend and a wonderful doctor. He'd fit perfectly into the Monroe family. He hadn't been the least bit arrogant, as she'd often wondered if Nick had been, before his injury.

She helped her mother navigate the stairs, wondering what Nick and her father were talking about. A wry laugh escaped. Oh, yeah, she had it bad. Hadn't she just lectured herself about getting over him? What was wrong with her? She hadn't felt this excited about seeing Shane when he'd hung around.

Maybe because Nick was an unknown entity, while Shane had been around seemingly forever. She felt certain that once she'd gotten to know Nick better, she wouldn't experience this weird anticipation about spending time with him anymore.

In the kitchen, she found Alec and Andrea were making dinner. Or, rather, Andrea was doing the work, while Alec directed activities from his seat at the kitchen table.

"It's about time you showed up." Alec scowled. "Mom was worried. Did you have to work late?"

Gritting her teeth, she flashed a tight smile. "What's the matter, Alec? Cranky because you didn't catch any bad guys last night?"

He ignored her dig. "What's the deal with this Nick guy you're seeing?" He pinned her with a narrow glare. "Fill me in."

"I'm not seeing him. He's a friend, in town temporarily. I thought it would be nice for him to have a home cooked dinner."

"Again? Two days in a row?" Andrea wiggled her eyebrows. "Hmm."

"Knock it off." This was why she wanted to leave, so she could simply live her life without having to deal with the constant opinions of her nosey family. She peered over Andrea's shoulder. "Your chicken salad looks good."

"Thanks." Andrea swiped her hands on a towel, then

handed her the bowl. "Please carry this into the dining room."

She did as Andrea asked. From the dining room, she could hear Nick and her father talking outside on the porch. She paused, blatantly eavesdropping on their conversation.

"No, sir," Nick was saying. "I don't have any family of my own. I grew up in foster homes and joined the army as soon as I graduated high school."

"How in the blazes did you manage to get into medical school?" Abe asked in an incredulous tone.

"I was blessed. They gave me a series of standard tests and realized I was brighter than my bad grades indicated." When he paused, she strained to listen. Nick sounded almost embarrassed. "Seems my greatest strength was science so after I did my first four year tour, I used the GI bill to attend college while staying in the Army reserves. Then I went on to medical school. His voice grew quieter. "The Army helped pay for that, so I had to give the government several years of my life working as a surgeon in the armed forces after I was finished with my residency. All in all, I was very fortunate. Without the army, I wouldn't be where I am today."

Stunned, she shivered at the depth of emotion in his voice. Nick had been raised in a series of foster homes, barely graduated from high school, and he thought he was lucky.

Many surgeons were arrogant, she'd even assumed Nick may have once been, too. But she was wrong, and now she knew why. His humble beginnings had made him the man he was today.

"Amber?" Her father's voice rose. "Would you please bring us a refill on our lemonade?"

"Sure." She set the bowl of chicken salad in the center

of the dining room table, and then went back into the kitchen for the pitcher of lemonade. Alec stood.

"When do I get to meet him?" Her goofball brother cracked his knuckles, pretending to be tough. "Does he know I carry a gun?"

"Ha ha. Very funny." Ignoring her brother's attempt at humor, she carried the pitcher of lemonade out to the porch where Nick and her father were sitting.

Her dad beamed. "Thanks, sweetheart. I'll tell you, Nick, I don't know what we're going to do once Amber is gone." Her father shook his head ruefully. "We've really come to depend on her."

"Gone?" Nick's gaze swiveled toward her, a frown puckered between his brows. "You mean, like taking a well deserved vacation?"

"No, I mean when she moves away." Her father didn't seem to notice Nick's startled expression. "Didn't she tell you? She's moving to Florida in a few weeks. Even has a job lined up down there." Her dad smiled and winked at her. "Do you know how many miles there are between Milwaukee and Fort Meyers? One thousand, three hundred and eighty-six. That's a really long way."

"Dad," she warned. Nick's dumbfounded expression twisted her stomach into a knot.

"No." Nick's tone was clipped. "She didn't tell me."

She stood there, unsure of what to say. She hadn't intentionally kept her plans a secret. But the faint accusation in his gaze told her he thought otherwise.

CHAPTER SIX

Nick's intense gaze throughout dinner robbed Amber of her appetite. There was no reason to feel lousy about not sharing her plans with him. They barely knew each other, and certainly didn't have a real close relationship.

This time together was just a brief interlude in their lives. In a few days, maybe a week at the most, they'd go their separate ways. Even if Nick took the temporary hospitalist position, he wasn't planning to stay in Milwaukee, forever. He would eventually return to whatever temporary base he called home and she'd finish her stint at the VA hospital then move on to her new job in Florida.

A sense of desolation crept over her. Her plan to move had seemed like such a great idea. Her brothers had lived in different states, Austin was still in California, Aaron in Boston, Massachusetts. Nick had lived all over the world. He hadn't been tied down by an overprotective family.

So why wasn't she happier at the idea of leaving?

"You were stationed in Germany for a year, then?" Abe addressed Nick. "How did you manage, without speaking the language?"

Nick shrugged as if embarrassed by all the attention to his life. "I picked up some of the language along the way. Most of our soldiers obviously are American, so it wasn't that big of a deal. But the German language wasn't as hard to learn as you might think." Then he grimaced and added, "Now Chinese? That's a much different ball game. Talk about a difficult language to figure out. The whole time I was in Beijing, I didn't learn much more than the words for hello, goodbye and bathroom."

She picked at her food, wishing the meal would end soon. Her parents listened to Nick with rapt attention. Strange, Shane had been so much a part of the family that her parents hadn't acted as if him being around was anything special. She found the way they fawned over Nick extremely irritating.

Finally, she stood and began clearing the table.

"Anyone want dessert?" Her mother asked.

"Thank you, but I'm full." Nick smiled. "The meal was wonderful, thanks for including me."

"Yeah," Alec agreed. "I'm stuffed, too."

"Mom, Dad, why don't you sit on the porch for a while? It's a beautiful evening," she said encouragingly. "We'll save your peach cobbler for later."

"I'd like that," her mother murmured. As her dad escorted her mother outside, Andrea went in search of her children. Beth and Ben had been excused early, since the adults had been busy talking. Or rather, hanging on Nick's every word, she thought with a grimace.

Alec sat for a minute, but when Nick stood and pitched in to help with the dishes, her brother made a quick escape. Apparently, his desire to keep an eye on their guest wasn't as keen as escaping the chore of taking care of the dishes.

Nick's movements were slow and stiff, making her

wonder if he had taken the medication they'd stopped to pick up from his motel room.

Eyeing him subtly, she noticed his lopsided gait was definitely more pronounced as she followed him into the kitchen. She gave a mild snort. Yeah. Take medication? Not likely.

"Where are your pain meds?" She set her load of dishes in the sink with the clatter. "You need to take them."

He scowled. "I'm fine." As if to prove it, he spun awkwardly around and went back to the dining room for more dishes.

Gnashing her teeth at his stubbornness, she began to rinse the glassware, then packed each item in the dishwasher. When he returned, she took the stack of plates from his hands.

"You're not fine. I don't get it. What is the big deal with taking the pain medication you so obviously need?"

"You're right. You don't get it at all." His eyes flashed and she was taken aback by his anger.

"It's all about your ego, isn't it?" She jammed the dishes into the dishwasher with far more force than necessary. He was acting just like her brothers. "Heaven forbid you should give in to any weakness."

She gasped when he spun her away from the dishwasher and hauled her against his hard frame. Her pulse quickened with anticipation.

"No, it's not about my ego."

This close she was immersed by the way his gray-green eyes glittered with flecks of gold around his dilated pupils. She splayed her hands over his chest, the muscles taut beneath her fingertips. She wished she could wrap her arms around his neck and kiss him even though she knew what would be playing with fire.

"Those pills create a foggy haze in my mind I detest. At least the jagged edges of pain help remind me I'm alive." His intense gaze dropped and lingered on her mouth. His voice dropped low. "It reminds me that being here like this, with you and your family, isn't a dream. That I won't wake up to find myself strapped in some strange hospital bed, reliving the nightmare of the plane crash."

Shaken, she stared at him. What horrors he must have gone through. The unguarded emotion in his gaze called to her on a completely different level. Unable to resist, she rose on tiptoe and gently pressed her lips against his. At first he seemed startled by her kiss, then in an instant he pulled her close and delved deep, as if he were a dying man given his last sip of water.

Then, just as abruptly, he pushed her away, his chest heaving as if he'd run ten miles. Without his arms supporting her, she stumbled back against the edge of the sink, dazed and wondering what had just happened.

"This isn't smart. I have to go." He limped away surprisingly fast and she couldn't do anything except listen as he said thanks and bade her parents good night before leaving.

She closed her eyes and rubbed a hand over her forehead. As much as she was sick and tired of this push me, pull me routine, one thing she could agree with.

Kissing him was not at all smart.

AMBER WORKED TWO GRAVEYARD SHIFTS, which was far from her favorite shift, then was more than happy to have a few days off. On her second day off, however, the shrill ringing of the phone woke her. She opened one bleary eye to see the hour was barely six in the morning. As much as she wanted to bury her head under the pillow, there was only one place that would be calling her so early.

With a muffled groan, she snagged her cell phone from the bedside table. "Hello?"

"Amber? This is the night supervisor at the hospital. We had a sick call this morning, would you mind coming in to help?"

Yeah, she minded, but bit back the automatic refusal. The extra money would come in handy when she moved to Florida. And she couldn't bear to think of their patients suffering while the nurses worked shorthanded. Repressing a sigh, she agreed. "Sure. But I might be a little late. You woke me up."

"Thanks so much. You're a lifesaver." The night supervisor disconnected from the call in a hurry, as if afraid she might change her mind.

A shower helped clear the sleepy fog from her brain. Thanks to Nick, sleep hadn't come easily. The irritating man had dominated her thoughts. In an effort to avoid dwelling on her irrational feelings for him, she'd visualized some of the happy times she'd spent with Shane. But for some reason she'd had trouble picturing Shane's smiling face. At midnight she'd crawled from her bed to scroll through her cell phone photos to help build a clearer picture in her mind.

Even then, most of her memories were centered around times they'd hung out as a family. Like when they'd all played tackle football the day after Thanksgiving. She, Shane and Adam had been on the same team. When Shane had lobbed a pass toward her, she'd caught it for the winning touchdown. He'd run after her, nearly tackling her in the process of enveloping her in a big hug to celebrate.

Shane had been known entity, and Nick was anything but. She only knew the bits and pieces of his life he'd shared with her and her family. She pulled on a clean set of scrubs, grabbed her stethoscope and headed outside to walk the few blocks to work. It had been distressing to realize how few times she and Shane had actually been alone. Truthfully, even the kiss he'd given her before leaving for Beijing was difficult to recall. Nick's searing, demanding kisses were so different, so clearly vivid in her mind, overshadowing her memories of Shane.

A fact she didn't like one bit. With a frown, she picked up her pace, knowing the later she was, the longer the night nurses waiting on her arrival would have to stay working overtime.

The rehab unit was hopping. Which was a good thing. Hard work had the great advantage of distracting her from thinking about Nick Tanner. She jumped in, taking a quick report on her patients then diving into work.

Just before lunch, one of the floors called to give report on a patient who had been accepted as a rehab transfer. Amber volunteered to take the new admission and asked one of the patient care assistants to get a room ready while she finished hanging an IV antibiotic.

The patient rolled in a half-hour later. The floor nurse had informed her the patient was Gerald Fisher, a 73-year-old man recovering from an ischemic stroke, the type caused by a blood clot. She entered his room with a bright smile. "Good morning, Mr. Fisher. How are you feeling?"

"Purple shoe. Shoe, purple shoe."

What? His earnest, compelling gaze convinced her he wasn't trying to be funny. She stepped closer, noticing how the pupil in his right eye was slightly larger than his left.

"Mr. Fisher, squeeze my fingers with your hands." She

tried not to show her concern, but she was worried he'd extended his stroke. Or his stroke hadn't resolved in the first place. How on earth had he been accepted for a transfer?

He took her fingers in his hands and squeezed. His right side was markedly weaker than his left. As she continued her assessment, she discovered he couldn't move his right leg at all. She knew this man needed immediate stroke care. "Don't move or try to get up, okay?"

She quickly used her hands free device around her neck to call for the Stroke Team. The team had been implemented a few years ago, and she was grateful for that, now. After putting that call through, she paged Dr. Roland, using the 911 preface that nurses used to alert the physician they needed a quick response.

Her hands-free phone rang a minute later. "This is Amber."

"You paged? Again?" Roland asked in a snide tone.

She ignored his biting sarcasm. "Yes. I'm here with Mr. Fisher and I believe he has extended his stroke. He's aphasic, his pupils are unequal. His right hand grasp is weaker than the left. He can't move his right leg at all. His blood pressure is 160/90, pulse is 104 and respirations are 16 per minute. He is not running a fever."

"He doesn't sound that much worse from when I accepted his transfer," Roland said, and she thought maybe his speech was slightly slurred. Or maybe she was just angry.

He'd actually accepted this patient in his current condition? A flash of anger burned as she moved further outside Mr. Fisher's room so he couldn't overhear.

She spoke professionally with an effort. "Dr. Roland, this patient is not stable for rehab. His neuro status is such, that I don't even think he should be on a regular unit. The stroke team is on their way. I believe he'll need to be trans-ferred to the ICU."

"Fine. Let the stroke team decide where he should go. And watch your tone," he added. "Or I'll get you written up for insubordination." Before she could say anything more, he disconnected from the call.

Insubordination? For informing him of his patient's worsening condition? Unbelievable. She swallowed her anger, and turned to walk back into Mr. Fisher's room, just as two staff members, a doctor and nurse, came running down the hall.

"Did you call the stroke team?" The nurse asked.

"Yes." Grateful to have expert reinforcements, she reit-erated Mr. Fisher's assessment. The grave expressions on both of their faces, made her feel better. She had not over-reacted about the seriousness of Mr. Fisher's condition.

The two members of the stoke team, quickly entered Mr. Fisher's room. Less than a minute later, they asked her to call for the transport team.

"We're taking him straight down to the CT scanner, then we'll secure a room for him in the neuro intensive care unit," the nurse said. "Depending on the result of his scan, he may go directly to the interventional radiology suite for another procedure."

"Understood." She quickly made the call, hoping Roland would show up as Mr. Fisher was being whisked away.

Then again, maybe it was better if Roland didn't show his face after all. She might not be able to hold back her opinion of his apathetic approach to patient care.

"Amber? Is something wrong?"

She spun around to find Nick standing beside her, wearing dress slacks and plaid shirt covered by a white lab coat. He had a stethoscope around his neck, and eyeing his name tag, she realized he'd taken the temporary hospitalist position. She hadn't seen him since the night he'd stayed for dinner at her parents' house and was irrationally irked at how handsome he looked.

"One of my patients isn't doing very well." She gestured toward Mr. Fisher's room, noticing the transport team had arrived. "Excuse me." She stepped away to help get Mr. Fisher transferred from the wheelchair to the gurney.

To her surprise, Nick followed. He frowned when Mr. Fisher continued saying, "Purple shoe." It wasn't unusual to have some patients use non sensical words when suffering an acute stroke. They could hear and understand, but couldn't pick the right words to say what they were feeling.

Amber had a bad feeling, purple shoe meant headache.

"When did this start?" Nick asked.

"He arrived from the inpatient nursing unit, like this." She glanced at her watch. "Less than fifteen minutes ago."

The scowl on Nick's features was reassuring. He was getting a taste of Dr. Roland's decision making right off the bat.

"Definitely acute stroke symptoms," he said. The pretty dark haired neurologist nodded in agreement.

"What's going on here?" Dr. Roland loomed in the doorway. She turned toward him. He was short, round, weighing at least three hundred pounds, and reeked of cigarette smoke, intermingled with another scent she couldn't quite place. He looked like a walking heart attack waiting to happen. And she was secretly glad she had both Nick and the stroke team members here to witness this conversation.

She lifted her chin, meeting his gaze head on. She would not cower in the face of his anger. "As I mentioned, I called the stroke team. They're here, now. And Dr. Tanner came over to see Mr. Fisher, too."

Roland's face flushed with anger, but after eyeing the other health care providers in the room, he didn't let loose the way she sensed he'd wanted to. "This patient must have taken a turn for the worse during his transfer."

It was all she could do not to throw the truth in his face. And from what she could tell, Nick felt the same way.

"In checking Mr. Fisher's chart, it appears these symptoms started prior to you accepting him as a rehab patient," Nick said in a curt voice. "This patient wasn't a candidate for rehab at all. I think you owe Ms. Monroe an apology."

Roland's face turned an alarming shade of purple. "You have no right to speak to me like that. Do you know who I am? I'm the medical director of this unit!"

"I know exactly who you are." Nick looked tall and imposing, even with his cane, as he stepped closer to the older man. "Do you know who I am? Nick Tanner, the new hospitalist. And I suggest you watch your tone, or we'll continue this conversation down in Rick Johnson's office."

The threat of being reported to the chief of staff was enough to have Roland backing down. He shot her a furious glare, then turned and stalked off toward the nursing station.

It was on the tip of her tongue to ask Roland if he planned to make rounds, but she decided against it.

With Nick here on the unit, she felt certain Roland would have to put forth an effort. She'd have to settle for that.

CHAPTER SEVEN

Nick had never been so furious with a colleague in his entire career. He wasn't prone to violence, but if Roland hadn't stormed off, presumably to actually do his job and make rounds on his patients, he actually might have punched the guy.

A temptation that would not have done his surgeons hands any good but would have gone a long way and making him feel better.

Pushing away his anger, he stepped aside to allow the neurologist and the nurse from the stroke team to push Mr. Fisher's gurney out of the room. Amber walked alongside, murmuring words of encouragement to her patient. He was impressed by the way she'd stood her ground with Roland. She might look like a fresh faced eighteen-year-old, all sweet and nice, but when she believed in something—lookout.

He knew one of the reasons he'd taken this role had been to stay close to her. Even if that was only for a short period of time. Oh, he still wanted to help, especially if there was a problem with patient care on the rehab unit. But the real reason he'd agreed to stay was far more complex. Amber stood a few feet down the hall, watching as Mr. Fisher was whisked away. Despite the seriousness of the situation, she turned and flashed a smile. "You were great. Thanks for being here."

"Of course." Her smile lit up her whole face, beaming warmth into his cold soul. He couldn't figure out how she did it, but just being in her presence made him feel better. Her patients no doubt loved her.

As Shane had? He rubbed a hand along the tense muscles on the back of his neck. Discovering her plan to move across the country had sent him reeling. He could completely understand the desire to start over someplace new. Had losing Shane factored into her decision to leave?

Most likely. His gut tightened with apprehension, and he quickly sidelined the thought before guilt could swallow him whole. Her reasons for leaving Milwaukee didn't matter one way or the other. Amber needed a friend and, as much as he hated to admit it, Shane wasn't here.

But that hadn't stopped *him* from arranging things so that *he* was.

Nick turned his attention back to the situation at hand. Roland wasn't the only physician responsible for this near catastrophe. The doctor who'd initiated the transfer off the acute care unit in the first place, was also at fault.

Not that he wanted to play the blame game. He knew full well nobody was perfect. However, this situation should be reviewed from a quality assurance perspective to prevent something like this from happening again. He went to the nurse's station, dropping behind the closest unoccupied computer and spent a few minutes reviewing Mr. Fishers chart. Multiple phone calls later, he'd gotten the information he needed.

"Did you find out why the floor transferred Mr. Fisher?" She stepped up beside him. Obviously, she'd been listening to his phone calls.

"Yeah." He sat back in his chair, massaging his left thigh with one hand. "The hospital is in a severe bed crunch. The resident hadn't seen Mr. Fisher since much earlier this morning, but heard how they had patients backed up in the emergency department. He basically made the decision to request a transfer to rehab, to free up a bed."

"And Dr. Roland accepted the patient."

"Yep. According to the resident, he gave Roland the symptoms he'd noticed earlier that morning, not anything more recent. Roland accepted the patient based on that information. As far as the resident knows, Roland never assessed the patient for himself. Or knew anything about his worsening neurologic symptoms."

Her brow furrowed. "Roland should have looked at Mr. Fisher 's chart prior to accepting the transfer. And the nurses on the floor should have recognized how much worse he was. They should have phoned the resident to stop the transfer. In fact, they should have called the stroke team, the way I did."

Nick shrugged. "Yeah, but if they were short staffed and knew they had to make room for other patients, they may not have taken the time to assess him very closely."

She sighed and shrugged. "I guess I can see how that could happen. At least Mr. Fischer is getting the care he needs now. I appreciate you supporting me with Roland."

"You're welcome." He wanted to say he'd always be there for her but of course that wasn't going to happen. Amber hurried off to take care of her other patients. No doubt the time she'd spent with Mr. Fischer had put her behind schedule.

Watching her go, Nick berated himself for being a fool.

He was far too emotionally involved with Amber Monroe. Sharing dinner with her family and watching as she took care of patients certainly wasn't going to help. He needed distance. Maybe taking this temporary hospitalist role hadn't been the smartest idea. Being this close to her on a daily basis, was not helping him.

He remained seated at the computer workstation, glad for the chance to take some of the pressure off his leg. He finished typing a brief note on Mr. Fischer in the patient's electronic record, then reviewed Amber's documentation as well. She'd stuck to the facts, without implicating Roland in any way. Very professional. He was glad she hadn't been tempted to call the man out in the legal medical record. Those conversations were best had one-on-one.

He stood to stretch, and then reached for his stethoscope. His fingers closed around the tubing but the heavy weight of the bell pulled it from his grasp, and it fell to the floor with a clatter. He stared at the stethoscope lying in a twisted heap, then shifted his gaze to his numb fingers. Anger lodged in his throat. He'd been fooling himself. When he had managed to intubate Amber's patient in the rehab gym, he'd figured the nerves and muscles in his fingers were getting better. But when the stethoscope began to fall, he hadn't even realized it slipped from his fingers.

The stark truth hit hard. His hand wasn't any better.

The nerve damage was likely permanent. The nerve specialist had tried to prepare him for this, but he hadn't wanted to believe it.

Outwardly he was calm as he bent to pick the stethoscope off the floor, but deep inside impotent rage beat against his chest. He took one deep breath, then another as he walked off the unit. No use thinking about his grim future.

Thankfully Amber had a future. She was a great nurse. She deserved to be happy, to travel wherever her heart desired. To start over and live the life of her dreams. Thinking about it now, he remembered sensing and underlying longing in her letters to Shane, but he hadn't completely understood the depth of her feelings until now.

I have this crazy impulse to hop an international flight to Beijing so I can visit you. Your descriptions of China are amazing. The Shanghai open market is easy to picture in my mind. I can practically hear the people chattering in rapid fire Chinese. I'm dying to see everything for myself. Or at least to see something outside of Wisconsin. Yet, the thought of traveling alone halfway across the world is a bit intimidating. I do it, though, for a chance to see China with you.

The idea of traveling halfway around the world alone hadn't bothered him at all. Once he would have been more than ready to drop everything and take off for a new adventure.

But not anymore.

Months of rehab, lying in his bed writhing in agony with no one to turn to other than the nurse currently assigned to him, had changed his whole perception of life. In his current condition, thrill seeking lacked appeal.

Not that he'd gone skydiving from planes, or bungee jumping off cliffs, but his entire lifestyle, from the time he had been a kid, had been that of a nomad moving restlessly from one place to another, always seeking something new.

He was tired of wandering from place to place. The one thing he'd longed for during the time of his injury recovery had been something he'd never had. Home. A family. A partner to share his life with.

For a brief moment upon crossing the threshold of the Monroe household, he'd imagined he'd found what he'd been looking for. He'd grown to care about Amber through her letters, but seeing her in person had been like touching a live wire. She radiated positive energy in a way he envied. Under different circumstances, he'd be more than a little tempted to push for something more. He couldn't get close to her without wanting to kiss her. Yet they both stood on opposite ends of the spectrum as far as their personal lives were concerned.

He had no future as a surgeon, no idea what he'd do with the rest of his life.

Amber had a wonderful career as a nurse, giving each of her patients the very best care possible. She'd devoted much of her time to her family, while Nick had only lived to please himself.

Here in Milwaukee, Nick had finally felt as if he'd come home.

While Amber had one foot out the door, ready to embark on her next adventure.

"ARE YOU FINISHED FOR THE DAY?" He met Amber's gaze when finally dropped into a chair behind the nurse's station. She'd been on her feet far more than he had been. He should have been as weary as she looked, but performing hospitalist consults on the various rehab patients had taken his mind off his own problems. So far, he hadn't seen anything out of the ordinary with any of the patient's medical care. Which was a good thing.

"I think so." She sighed. "Mr. Fischer was taken from the CT scanner to the interventional radiology suite for another procedure to remove the clot causing his stroke symptoms. From there he's being transferred to the ICU.

That makes two ICU transfers in the nine days. Highly unusual for us."

"Hey, it's not your fault." He resisted the urge to smooth a stray strand of her reddish blonde hair from her cheek. She looked tired, worn out, especially after her interaction with Roland. She'd been so busy taking care of everyone else, maybe it was time for someone to take care of her? He cleared his throat. "Do you have plans for this evening?" *Smooth, Tanner. Really smooth.*

She didn't seem to notice his poor transition from the professional to the personal. "This was supposed to be my day off." She grimaced and glanced at her watch. "Thankfully, my shift today is considered overtime."

"How would you like to go out for dinner? Someplace special, like DiCarlo's downtown."

A flare of pleasure lit her gaze, then almost instantly faded. "Thanks, but I'm pretty tired. It's been a long day."

The way her gaze slid from his convinced him she was lying through her teeth. As if she'd wanted to go to dinner then had made-up the old, I'm-too-tired excuse. Clearly the problem was that she didn't want to go with him.

His fault, for sending mixed signals. In fact, his signals were so jumbled it was as if they'd been strewn throughout his body by a tornado. They wanted different things from life, but maybe just for tonight they could find a way to meet in the middle. For some reason, he just couldn't quite let her go. Besides, he wanted a chance to ask her a little more about Roland. As long as they kept things friendly, what was the harm?

She was messing with his head, but he didn't care. He swallowed a self-depreciating grimace. So much for thinking he'd given up his thrill-seeking behavior.

"Please?" Nick kept his voice low, although there wasn't

anyone else around to overhear them. "You deserve a nice dinner after the day you've put in."

She arched her brow. "Is that the only reason I should go?"

"No. You should come because I enjoy spending time with you." Admitting the bald truth wasn't as hard as he'd thought. Besides, whether she realized it or not, between her family and work, she needed an evening away. And he wanted to be the guy sharing it with her.

She was quiet for so long he figured he'd struck out. Again.

"Just to be clear, you're asking me out? Like on a date?" She toyed with the simple gold crucifix hanging around her neck.

"Yes." He swallowed hard. When she stated the word so bluntly, he felt nervous. When was the last time he'd had a date? He couldn't remember. The women in his past were a total blur. "I'll pick you up at seven."

"You don't have a car," she protested.

"Seven," he repeated. "Don't worry about me, just be ready to go at seven."

"All right." She stood, a hesitant smile tugging at her mouth. "I guess I'll see you later, then."

He nodded then forced himself to leave. But as he walked back to his motel room across the street, the swell of anticipation made his heart race. He placed a hand over the center of his chest and pressed hard. *Cool it, Tanner. You're treating Amber to a nice dinner because she deserves it. Keep things light and friendly and you'll do fine.*

He could only hope the stern lecture prevented him from doing something he would regret. Like kissing her again.

AMBER HAD the whole house to herself. She did a little dance as she headed up the stairs. Because of her last minute call in to work, her sister Andrea had invited her parents to have dinner at her house. Adam was on call. Alec was doing some sort of special SWAT team training. Thankfully none of her annoying siblings were around to ply her with questions about her plans for the evening.

At times like this, she really, really missed her apartment. Even with Alec living one floor above her. Still, helping her parents wasn't the end of the world. Only a few more weeks until she was out on her own again.

Far, far away in another state. Where no one could drop in at a moment's notice to spy on her or make her feel stupid and inept.

She jumped in the shower, intent on rinsing thoughts of her family from her mind. Unbelievable that Nick had actually asked her out on a real date. As she massaged shampoo through her hair, she couldn't prevent the thrill of anticipation. The same, rational part of her brain wondered if this was just another of his push me, pull me moves. One minute he kissed her, the next he'd shoved her away. Now he'd asked her out. Because he knew she planned to move to Florida? Maybe Nick assumed she wouldn't ask for anything more than what he could give.

The thought made her pause. Was that what this was about. Was he sick of sitting around his motel room? Maybe this was nothing more as a way for him to get away for a while. He'd asked her because he knew her. And why did that idea bother her? It wasn't like they could have a serious relationship. She was leaving, and he probably would too.

He'd mentioned his boss in Virginia. She felt certain Nick would end up back there.

Her feelings about him were a tangled mess. Why she was letting herself be distracted by a guy she wouldn't see again, she had no idea.

Then again, maybe there was more to her confused emotions. Most of the guys she'd met had only seen her as the friendly girl next door. Aaron's cute little sister. Adam's cute little sister. Or Alec's cute little sister. Or...

Not Nick. When he looked at her through those intense gray-green eyes of his, she didn't feel like the wholesome girl next door at all. Oddly he seemed to consider her an attractive woman. Or was that just wishful thinking? After all, at their first meeting, he'd assumed she was much younger than she actually was.

After stepping out of the shower she dried off then hurried into her room. She contemplated the items in her closet. It had been so long since she'd been out on a date, she didn't have dressy clothes to wear.

There was one outfit that she hadn't worn in over a year. A flowered blue green skirt, along with the spaghetti strapped camisole top. She dressed then regarded herself critically in the mirror. Her skirt flared when she gave a quick spin, showing off her tanned legs, one of her best features, if she did say so herself. At least tonight, she wouldn't look like a sixteen-year-old.

She was still fussing with her hair and makeup when she heard the doorbell ring. She smoothed a hand over her skirt, then headed downstairs. Nick stood straight and tall on the other side of the screen door. His eyes flared with interest and he smiled with appreciation when he saw her. "Hello Amber. You look lovely."

"Thank you." She shouldn't have sounded so breathless.

He politely opened the door, but she didn't invite him in. "I'm ready if you are. My parents aren't home, or I'd invite you in to say hello. They're at Andrea's house." She stepped out onto the wide wrap around porch, brushing past him.

"You smell great, too. "He lightly clasped her arm then turned to maneuver the porch steps with his cane and his awkward gait. "We have reservations for seven-thirty. I hope you're hungry."

Normally she would be, but her nerves had taken control of her stomach. She nodded to the black car parked outside the house. "I'm impressed you rented a car just for this."

"You're worth it." His simple statement shot through her heart like an arrow, stealing her breath. "And, in case you're wondering, I haven't taken any meds for over four hours. I'm fine to drive."

She frowned, not liking the thought of him being in pain. "Are you sure that's a good idea? I mean about the pain meds, that is. I can drive. Or we can call a rideshare."

"I'm backing off on my meds anyway, remember?" His tone was light, but his arched brow and flint expression in his eyes warned her to leave it alone.

She settled in the front seat and waited for him to go around to join her. When he'd stashed his cane in the back and settled in behind the wheel she asked, "Did you happen to hear anything more about Mr. Fischer?" She almost hated to ask, concerned her patient was going to end up passing away, just like Mr. Goetz had. "I've been curious about how he's doing."

Nick pulled away from the curb, then reached over the gear shift in the center console to cover her hand with his. "I called the hospital for a status report just before I left. He's doing fine. The interventional radiology procedure has taken care of his symptoms. He's still in intensive care and has been deemed to be in critical but stable condition."

"I'm so glad." She sighed in relief.

"Me, too."

Fifteen minutes later, Nick pulled up to the restaurant. At first she was surprised he would use the valet parking, then remembered his cane. She was so accustomed to seeing him walk with it now, she didn't even notice it.

Their table was tucked in a secluded corner with a breathtaking view of Lake Michigan. The lake was east of Milwaukee, so there were no beautiful sunsets, but the rippling blue water was soothing all the same. The ambiance of the restaurant was warm and inviting. Fancier than she'd expected, too, making her glad she'd worn a dress.

"How about some antipasti for starters?" Nick asked, scanning the menu.

"Sounds great." She already knew exactly what she wanted from the menu—reading the description of the grilled swordfish made her mouth water.

A discreet waiter took their order. Classical music played in the background. Nick reached across the table to take her hand in his, pinning her with an intense gaze. "I need to ask you a question."

Her mouth went dry and she nervously licked her lips. Was he going to ask her to not move to Florida, to stay so they could see each other again? She managed to pull herself together. "Yes? What is it?"

His lean fingers lightly stroked her hand. She shivered. But then he pulled away, to reach for his water glass. "I'm curious about what action you're planning to take against Dr. Roland."

She blinked. "What?"

"I heard the way he spoke to you, Amber." He frowned

darkly from across the table. "Surely, you're not going to let that slide without taking some sort of formal action against him, are you? Every VA hospital has strict rules about professional conduct."

She couldn't believe that he'd only asked her out to grill her about Roland. She struggled to remain calm. "I'd rather not think about him, if you don't mind."

Her attempt to change the subject didn't work. He leaned earnestly over the table toward her. "I can help, I overheard the whole thing."

"I don't believe this." She sat back in her chair and glared at him.

He frowned eyeing her warily. "What do you mean? What's wrong?"

"What's wrong?" She stood and swept her hand over her skirt. "Did you notice how I'm dressed? Do you remember asking me out to dinner because I deserve to be pampered after such a stressful day?"

Wordlessly, he nodded.

"Then why are you badgering me about Roland? Are you so blind that you can't see what's sitting right in front of you?"

"Amber." He stood using the table for leverage instead of his cane. "Calm down. Of course, I see you. I told you how lovely you looked, remember?"

He had, but she couldn't seem to find her usual calm demeanor and didn't care if they were attracting attention from the rest of the patrons in the restaurant. "I didn't come here tonight to talk about work. I thought you wanted to get to know me better. But apparently I was wrong." She reached behind her to grab her purse.

"I—wait a minute, where are you going?"

"Home." Maybe she was overreacting but she'd really

thought this might be the beginning of something more. So much for her idiotic, romantic notions of thinking a guy like Nick might actually like her for herself.

"Don't go, please. I'm sorry. I didn't mean to focus on work. I—of course want to get to know you better." He sounded confused, as if he truly hadn't anticipated her reaction.

She stared at him for a long moment, unsure of what she should do. Staying was probably a bad idea. Even if they shared a nice evening together, where would it lead?

Absolutely nowhere.

CHAPTER EIGHT

"Please." Nick held her gaze. "You're right, I was trying to use work to keep you at arm's length."

She blinked as if stunned he'd admitted it. "Why?"

His chest tightened, but he wouldn't lie. "Because I like you, too much. And I know you're leaving town in a few short weeks."

Her shoulders slumped as her flare of annoyance appeared to fade away. She nodded thoughtfully, lowering her gaze to the table. "I see."

Did she? Because he wasn't so sure he did. Especially now. Seeing her dressed up and looking more stunning than ever had hit him hard. Maybe if things were different...

But they weren't.

He was far too aware of the curious glances they'd garnered from the others in the restaurant. He wasn't sure what to do. Take her home? Convince her to stay?

Their waiter hurried over, his expression anxious. "Is something wrong? Have you changed your mind about having dinner?"

Nick held out a hand toward her, palm upward. "Amber? Will you please stay for dinner?"

Her cheeks flushed, she nodded and returned to her seat. He almost laughed when he heard an audible sigh of relief from the waiter. Crisis averted.

"Some wine? Champagne perhaps?" The waiter asked as if hoping to soothe the tension between them.

"No thanks. I'll stick with water." Her tone was casual, and he couldn't quite figure out what she was thinking.

"I'll stick with water too." He eyed her carefully across the table. "Thanks for staying." He would have followed her out, but his body would have suffered for it. For the first time in a long time, he was physically hungry. "After losing so much weight in the hospital, I don't like to skip meals. I need every ounce of protein I can get."

A tiny frown puckered her brow as she digested his words. "I wouldn't want to be responsible for making you skip dinner, so you're welcome."

"I'm glad." Their antipasti arrived in less than sixty seconds. Almost as if the waiter thought that speed would help keep them there for the entire meal.

"This looks amazing." She smeared a bit of sweet tomato relish on a cracker then daintily took a bite. He averted his gaze so he wouldn't think about kissing those sweet lips. He tried their appetizer too and couldn't help but agree. One thing about DiCarlos's cuisine, he didn't have to remind himself to eat. Focusing only on taking in enough protein to repair his injured muscles.

"Tell me what made you decide to work in Fort Meyers, Florida?"

Her gaze looked thoughtful. "For one thing, it's far enough away from Milwaukee that my overprotective brothers can't follow me."

He cocked a brow. "That's really a concern? Your family seems very nice. I feel like there's more to your desire to get away than just your siblings."

She nodded. "Okay, you're right. I'm looking for something new, different. Maybe even a bit of adventure. I've always wanted to travel, maybe because I watched my older siblings leave to follow their dreams."

"I can understand that," he agreed. "I joined the army to get away from the never-ending myriad of foster homes." He shrugged. "I may have gotten a little more than I initially bargained for."

She frowned. "You're saying I'll regret leaving?"

"No, that wasn't what I meant at all," he hastened to reassure her. "But as a nurse, you know very well that the grass isn't always greener on the other side of the fence."

"True." She sat back as their waiter removed their empty appetizer plate. "But that's part of the adventure, isn't it? Not knowing what's behind the next corner? Or what's on the other side of the fence?"

"Yes." He took a sip of his water, reminding himself not to rain on her parade. He'd been just like her, once. He'd joined the Army, then taken the leap to attend college while being in the reserves. He'd taken many risks without a problem. Until the one that had nearly cost him his life. Yet if someone warned him four months ago against taking charter a tourist plane trip over the Great Wall of China, he'd have scoffed at them. Not when he'd been determined to see the amazing views from a small airplane.

Their meal arrived, looking, and smelling delicious. Sultry tastes exploded on his tongue, from the sweet asparagus to the rare grilled tuna dipped in a tangy soy sauce.

Food had never tasted so good. And he wasn't sure if

that was due to DiCarlos's amazing chef or because he was sharing the meal with Amber.

Probably both.

"The swordfish is delicious." He was pleased she seemed to be enjoying the meal as much as he was. She lifted her fork toward him. "Would you like to taste?"

As if mesmerized, he leaned forward to take the tidbit she'd offered. His gaze clung to hers. "Amazing," he murmured. Referring to her, more so than the swordfish.

"My travel nurse assignment is only for three months. If I don't like Fort Meyers, I can go somewhere else." She shrugged. "It may sound silly, but I had planned to visit as many states as my nursing license will allow."

Like physicians, nursing licenses were issued by the state where they'd taken their state boards. However, many states had reciprocity, meaning they would accept another state's license without requiring the licensee holder to retake their specific state boards. "I don't think it's silly at all," he said softly. "I can understand the desire to do something different."

"It's a little bit like what you're doing," she said.

"Me?" He frowned.

"Yes. You're still recuperating but took on the job of being a temporary hospitalist anyway. And that's a completely different role than what you were trained for, right?"

He grimaced. "It wasn't by choice. This happens to be the only role I can take at the moment."

She looked as if she wanted to say more, but their waiter approached. "How is everything tasting?"

"Wonderful." Amber beamed up at him. "Thank you."

"Excellent," he added.

"Dessert?" The waiter asked, hopefully.

"Not for me, thanks." She held up her hand. "Tempting, but I couldn't possibly eat another bite."

"No dessert for me, either." He felt as if just being here with Amber was enough of a treat.

The ride back to her parents' place didn't take long. He was ridiculously happy that he'd rented a car for the evening. Even though his leg was killing him without the pain meds, it was well worth it.

He slid out from behind the wheel, and decided not to use his cane when he walked around to open her door. As she slid out from her seat, she looked up at him.

"You never mentioned how you got those scars."

His gut clenched. "You didn't ask."

She licked her lips, then trailed her fingertip down the scar that was visible on his left forearm. "You were in the same plane crash as Shane, weren't you."

He'd known this moment would come, and realized he couldn't hide from the truth any longer. "Yes." Admitting the truth helped ease the burden of guilt sitting on his shoulders like a boulder. The cool evening breeze did not make him feel any better. "We were both in the plane when it crashed. Only I lived and he died."

And he still didn't know why God had chosen to take Shane, while letting him live.

———

AMBER STARED for a long moment at the jagged scar marring Nick's forearm. "I guess I didn't ask because I really didn't want to think about it. I didn't want to imagine the details of how Shane died."

Nick stood ramrod straight, looking as if he wanted to

be anywhere else but standing here on the sidewalk outside her parents' home. With her.

She took a deep, cleansing breath. From the moment she'd met Nick, Shane had become the least of her concerns. The deep scars Nick carried, inside and out, had caught her off guard. Imagining the extent of his wounds, the trauma Nick had lived through, was more upsetting than she'd anticipated. And those were the only details she cared about, the ones that had impacted this man standing before her.

"What happened?" She lightly stroked the jagged scar on his arm. For some odd reason, she sensed he needed to tell the story.

He leaned against the car, as if his leg couldn't bear his weight. "It was my fault. My idea." He stared down at the pale skin of her hand on his arm. As if he couldn't bear to meet her gaze. "I convinced Shane we needed to hire a small private plane in order to appreciate the whole, winding view of the Great Wall of China."

She remembered how she'd written to Shane about wishing she could have been there to see that amazing sight with him.

"Of course, the fact that we couldn't speak a word of Chinese didn't seem to matter. Why should I be concerned with actually communicating with the pilot of our plane?"

His biting sarcasm flayed her already aching heart. "I knew Shane, remember? Trust me. You didn't make him do anything he didn't want to do."

Nick continued as if he hadn't heard her. "We weren't in the air more than fifteen to twenty minutes when I noticed we were losing altitude. Suddenly we were heading straight toward a huge ridge of trees. I screamed at the pilot to pull up the nose and hit the throttle, but he didn't speak

English any better than we spoke Chinese. We skimmed along the tops of the trees and for a minute I thought we were going to make it out of there. But then a branch caught the wing of the plane tipping us sideways. Next thing I knew, we'd slammed into a tree, nose first. The plan was wedged in the branches. My side of the craft took the brunt of the damage. I was sitting behind the pilot."

She swallowed the lump in her throat. She could envision the crash so clearly. And her heart ached for what he'd gone through.

"I believe the pilot died on impact. Or maybe even went unconscious before the plane lost control—who knows? Shane was able to climb out of the wreck but... I couldn't. I was pinned in the plane up against the tree." He pulled away from her touch and scrubbed his hands over his face as if trying to obliterate the memory. "Shane wanted to stay with me but his cell phone wouldn't pick up a signal. I told him to walk away from the wreck, to find a place where he could call for help. But he wouldn't listen."

He paused and she held her breath, waiting for him to finish the story.

"Shane stayed with me. He climbed out on the branch, trying to pull it away so I might be able to break free. Then something snapped, and Shane fell, hitting the ground. A moment later, a large chunk of the plane broke free and dropped directly on top of him."

"Oh, Nick." She stepped closer, intent on giving him a hug, but he remained stiff and unyielding.

"I could see him lying on the ground beneath me, the chunk of metal sitting squarely on his chest." He stared into space, reliving the horror. "I called out to him the whole time I struggled to get out. No matter how hard I shoved against the metal pinning me in place, I couldn't seem to make it budge. I'm not sure how long I worked at it, but eventually I squeezed past to escape the wreckage."

He finally turned his head to meet her gaze. "I fell to the ground and crawled to Shane, but I was too late. He was already dead."

She felt bad for Shane but felt even worse for Nick. Hearing what he'd gone through, was difficult. He'd suffered as much if not more than Shane had. Praying she sounded calmer than she felt, she asked, "How on earth did you manage to get rescued?"

"Shane's cell phone, believe it or not. He must have dropped it when he fell and somehow it escaped being smashed by the chunk of plane. I crawled through the woods until I reached a clearing and was able to get a signal." He glanced away. "If I had worked harder to convince him to leave to get away from the plane, he'd be alive today."

"And if the situation were reversed, if Shane had been pinned in the wreck, would you have left him?" She reached up and pressed the palm of her hand over his chest. Over his heart. "I don't think so."

"Maybe not." He still didn't meet her gaze. "Regardless, it was my stupid idea. I chartered the plane. Hired the idiot who couldn't fly."

"I'm sure the view of the wall was breathtaking."

"It wasn't worth Shane's life." He brushed her hand away from his chest, as if her touch seared him. "So now you know the truth. That I was the one that should have died in the crash, not Shane. I should have told you every-thing right from the beginning."

"It doesn't matter." She paused then added, "I appre-ciate your honesty but I'm very glad you're here."

He ignored her. "I was airlifted to Walter Reed hospital

in DC. A box of my belongings was shipped back but whoever packed it intermingled Shane's stuff with mine. That's how I ended up with your letters and copies of your emails. I made it my mission to bring them back to you."

"I'm glad." Looking at him now, her outrage at how he'd read them seemed petty. Nick had nearly died. Her mind couldn't seem to wrap itself around that horrifying fact. "I don't mind."

He gave her a strange look. "You were upset before, what changed now?"

She thought about that for a moment. "I guess I finally realized that it's more important that you're here now, alive and well."

He shook his head, as if he didn't quite believe her. He pushed away from the car, stepping carefully around her. "I'll walk you to the door."

"Great." She wished this evening could have ended differently. She tried to think of a way to regain the closeness they'd shared at dinner. On the porch, she turned to face him. "Thanks for dinner. I had a wonderful time."

He stared at her for a moment, his gaze shadowed. Then a flicker of exasperation crossed his features. "Why aren't you angry or upset with me? I know how much you cared about Shane. Your letters revealed the depth of your feelings."

She supposed she should feel embarrassed at how Nick had glimpsed into her heart, but she couldn't summon up the emotion. The girl who'd written those letters to Shane, had changed. She tipped her head to the side. "You're right about how much I cared for Shane. He was almost like a member of our family. But do you honestly think I place a higher value on his life than I do yours?"

"You should. He was a good man. Loyal to a fault."

Nick scowled. "He cared enough about you to save your letters."

"I know that now." She couldn't help but smile. Knowing Shane had saved her letters and emails helped ease the pain of losing him, at least a little. "He was a great guy, and we had some nice video chats. But I preferred writing letters, it was easier to put my feelings into words on paper than to tell him face to face."

Nick nodded solemnly. "I can understand that."

"Shane was a great guy, but we can't go back and change the past. God chose to take Shane home. It's not up to us to question why."

He hesitated. "You really believe that?"

"I do." She touched the cross at her neck. "Knowing Shane is in a better place helps ease the pain of losing him."

"I wish I could share your conviction." His gaze clung to hers. "All those months in the hospital, unable to feed myself or get to the bathroom under my own power, I kept wondering, why me? Why did Shane die instead of me?"

"God has a reason for saving you, Nick."

He sighed and then shrugged. "Maybe, but I'm not much use in my current condition. I may be out of the hospital, but I am far from being healed. I may never be able to return to the operating room. And if that's true, I have no clue what I'm going to do with the rest of my life."

She caught his hand as he turned away. She didn't want him to leave like this. "Nick, wait." She stepped closer and leaned up to kiss him. He turned so that her kiss brushed his cheek, rather than landing on his mouth the way she'd intended.

"I have to go. Goodbye, Amber."

Goodbye. Not goodnight. Helpless, she could only watch him leave.

CHAPTER NINE

Amber walked to work the following morning, hoping the fresh air would combat her exhaustion. Last night, Nick's rejection of so much as a kiss, hurt more than she'd thought possible. She hadn't been able to sleep, because she'd enjoyed their dinner so much, only to have the evening end on a sour note.

When she had finally fallen asleep, her dreams had been just as exhausting. She'd dreamed she was at work where Shane and Nick were both patients of hers and she'd had to run from one to the other, trying to help them both as they cried out in pain, but succeeding in helping neither.

The quietness of the morning was a blessing. Taking a deep breath helped clear the sleepy fog from her mind. The summer day was a perfect seventy degrees. Too bad she had to go into work. Would she see Nick today? It was ridiculous how badly she wanted to.

When she walked onto the rehab floor, there was no sign of him. Silly to be disappointed, especially since it was early. No surprise he wasn't here yet. Most of the physicians didn't show up until well after 8:00 AM for their morning rounds.

Except for Roland, who didn't show up much at all.

"Hi," Irene greeted her. "I hate to tell you we're short-handed, down one nurse because Rachel called in sick again today."

She stifled a groan. "Okay, it's nothing we haven't worked through before. Did we at least get an extra nursing assistant?"

"Yes, thankfully we did."

"Good. We'll have to take seven patients apiece, and each nurse will have their own nurses aid to help." She stared at the census board, trying to figure out the fairest way to split up the various patient assignments.

Ten minutes later, they had divvied up the patients and had scattered for bedside shift report. Once that was finished, Amber started her day making rounds of the newer patients she didn't know very well. She took her time assessing them so she wouldn't miss anything. Mr. Fischer's acute stroke symptoms remained far too fresh in her memory.

By mid-morning she was feeling pretty good about being caught up with her work.

"Amber?"

She spun around when Irene called her name. "Yes?"

"Your patient, Mr. Cooper, is down in PT, requesting additional pain medication. The therapist just called up asking if you'd bring him down more."

She nodded. "I know Mr. Cooper has had a few rough days lately. Will you keep an eye on my patients for me? This shouldn't take too long."

"No problem."

She remembered the last time she'd gone down to the

gym, when poor Mr. Goetz had suffered his seizure. As she took the stairs down to the first floor, she wondered if Roland even realized Mr. Goetz had died. Or if he even cared.

She found Mr. Cooper using the parallel bars, trying to walk with his new prosthesis. He had lost one leg due to problems with circulation and he often complained of phantom pain in that leg. It was a common phenomenon, suffered by young soldiers, and those who were more elderly. Once Mr. Cooper had mastered walking with the new prosthesis, he'd be able to return home.

"Hi Mr. Cooper. Here's the pain medication you requested." A female physical therapist by the name of Emily stood nearby, watching to make sure Mr. Cooper didn't fall. She handed him the paper cup with the pill in it then said, "I'll get you some water, then let you get back to work."

She turned and caught sight of Nick, lifting weights with his injured leg on the weight room equipment located on the other side of the gym. His green T-shirt was damp with sweat, clinging to his chest and biceps as he fought against the resistance of the weights. Another physical therapist hovered nearby, keeping an eye on him.

After supplying Mr. Cooper with his water, she smiled and approached Nick. He stared at a spot on the wall behind her and made soft grunting noises as he lifted his leg up then down.

"Hey, how are you," she greeted him. "Are you heading up to the unit later?"

He didn't smile, barely looked at her to even acknowledge she was standing there. With a slight nod he continued to remain totally focused while he exercised his muscles like a man possessed.

She wasn't sure if he'd responded to her question or had simply acknowledged her presence, but clearly, he was too preoccupied for conversation. Swallowing a flare of disappointment, she turned away, leaving Nick to face his demons alone.

Upstairs, Irene was having a tough time working with the social worker to have one of her patients transferred to a nursing home. For the next several hours, Amber was too busy to agonize over Nick.

She finally sat at the computer to complete her documentation when she heard a loud thunk.

What was that? She jumped to her feet and hurried to the room directly across from the nurse's station, where the emergency light was flashing.

Blood splatters stained the walls, the sheets of the bed, the linoleum and the patient lying on his side on the floor near the foot of the bed. The bed alarm shrilled loudly, and she snapped it off then fell to her knees beside her patient her heart and her throat. "Mr. Krantz! What happened?"

"Ohh," he groaned and rolled onto his back. Dark brown stains smeared his sweatpants.

"Oh, no, you had diarrhea again, didn't you? You poor thing." She knew Mr. Krantz continued to be plagued by these episodes where he needed to get to the bathroom in a hurry. But the diarrhea didn't explain where all the blood had come from.

"Please stay still, don't move." She placed a hand on his arm to hold him in place. Then she reached up to her portable phone. "Page Dr. Roland."

"Paging Dr. Roland," the mechanical voice repeated.

Of course the guy didn't answer. She left a terse message. "Mr. Krantz fell. Please come up to the unit right away." She ended the call, then raised her voice to be heard in the hallway, "Wendy? See if there are any physicians on the floor. Mr. Krantz fell on the floor."

"Okay."

She turned her attention back to her patient. The cut on his forehead had bled, but not much. She moved down to the red spot on his hospital gown and found it. He must have gotten his hand tangled in his IV tubing and pulled it out.

She glanced back over her shoulder. The tail end of the IV catheter was lying in his bed, where the linens soaked up the medication that should have been going into his veins.

"Mr. Krantz, wiggle your fingers and toes for me." She was afraid to move him in case he'd fractured his hip or his spine. Leaving him on the floor though, bothered her. She threw an impatient glance toward the doorway. What was taking Roland so long? "Tell me what hurts."

"My hip. I landed on it funny." The older gentleman's eyes were full of apology. "I know I was supposed to call first, but I didn't think there would be enough time..."

"Shh, it's okay. Don't worry, we'll get you cleaned up and off the floor in a jiffy." She felt bad for the poor man. Wendy and Irene rushed in, carrying a long backboard.

Between the three of them, they carefully log rolled Mr. Krantz onto the backboard and then lifted him up onto the bed. Amber sent Wendy for a fresh patient gown and sheets so they could get the worst of the blood and diarrhea cleaned up.

"What happened?" Nick's deep voice made her glance over in surprise. What was he doing here? After his mute act in the physical therapy gym, she assumed he had the day off. But here he was, freshly showered, wearing a green shirt and gray slacks rather than his sweaty gym clothes.

"I'm afraid Mr. Krantz tried to get up by himself to go to

the bathroom while he was getting his IV antibiotic. He fell, hit his head on the floor, and may have fractured his hip." She paused, then added, "He also pulled out his IV.

Nick's brows drew together in a concerned frowned. "Where does he hurt the most?"

"His hip. But I think he'll need his several X-rays to be sure. Maybe of his spine, pelvis and hip. We will need to replace his IV before he goes to radiology unless you think it's okay to wait until after."

"We need that IV in now, as I plan to order a CT scan of his head, too. And he'll need IV contrast for that." Nick frowned, peering at the older man's arms. "Doesn't look like he has great peripheral access. I think it would be better to place a central line."

She thought that was a good plan. "I'll call the radiology procedure area to see if they have an empty room and someone available to place the central line."

"I can replace the line, so don't worry about that." Nick spoke with confidence.

"Are you sure?" She didn't know if placing a central line was part of a hospitalist's duties or not.

"Yes, I'm credentialed to place central lines."

She nodded. Obviously, Mr. Krantz needed care, and if Nick was willing to place the line, she wasn't about to complain. Besides, there was no sign of Roland. And the sooner Mr. Krantz got the care he needed, the better.

"Can you help prepare Mr. Krantz for the central line placement?" Nick met her gaze. "I need the kit, drapes, and a new IV bag and tubing."

"Of course." She smiled, trying to reassure Mr. Krantz as he shot her a worried gaze. "I'll get the supplies right away."

She opened the central line kit and set out the supplies

for Nick to use. As he bathed Mr. Krantz's skin with the antiseptic solution she prepared a brand new IV. As Nick attempted to place the line, she logged into the computer, and began completing some of her paperwork.

But after just ten minutes Nick stepped away from Mr. Krantz's bedside, pushing the procedure table aside with his foot. "I'm sorry Mr. Krantz, I'm going to get someone to assist in getting this line in. I'll be right back. Are you doing, okay? "

"Yeah. Fine." Mr. Krantz's voice was faint.

She logged off the computer and went to his side. "I'm here Mr. Krantz. Do you need anything?"

"My hip hurts."

She nodded then met Nick's gaze. "How about giving him some pain medication?"

"Sure. Does he have any ordered?"

"Yes, he does." She had just accessed his record and the Percocet order was still valid.

"Great. Give him whatever he already has ordered."

She ducked out of Mr. Krantz's room to head over to the medication dispensing machine located on every nursing unit. After withdrawing the medication, she returned to Mr. Krantz's bedside. Mr. Krantz gratefully swallowed the pain med.

A moment later a second physician entered the room. He introduced himself as Dr. Jericho. She was surprised when Dr. Jericho had the central line placed in less than five minutes.

Nick returned to the room. "I submitted the orders for the radiology procedures. The transport team will be up here any minute."

"Sounds good." She gently patted Mr. Krantz's arm, the pain medicine already seeming to work as he smiled at her.

As Nick had promised, the transport team arrived a few minutes later.

After Mr. Krantz was wheeled down to radiology, she followed Nick to the physician's workroom. The space was empty, and the closed expression on his face told her he was still upset at not being able to place the line.

"Hey, it's no big deal. I'm sure he's a difficult access patient."

"That's not it." He glared at her. "Didn't you see how easy it was for Jericho to insert the line?"

She shrugged, not understanding what his problem was. "In my experience, some catheters go in easy, and some don't. I've had trouble placing an IV, only for another nurse to get it in right away. It's not that big of a deal."

"The problem wasn't with Mr. Krantz. The problem was with me." Nick opened and closed his hands. "My dexterity wasn't good enough to place one measly central line. I guess that's proof that returning to surgery is out of the question." His expression turned grim. "For good."

She didn't know what to say. She couldn't imagine what she would do if someone told her she couldn't be a nurse anymore.

But, then again, Nick was still a doctor. Just because he couldn't do surgery, didn't mean there was no hope of having a medical career.

"Can you treat trauma patients from a medical perspective while staying out of surgery?"

"No." His denial was swift.

She tried again. "I can imagine working as a trauma surgeon is exciting, but there's a lot of patient death, too, isn't there?"

"Sometimes. But there's nothing like the adrenaline rush of knowing there's an unstable trauma on its way in.

There's a challenge in taking someone extremely broken and putting them back together again."

"I can see your point. But do you know what I like most about rehab?"

Nick didn't answer.

"These patients have gotten through the worst of their traumatic injury and now they're on their way home. For the most part they're able to communicate with me. They are anxious to learn how to take care of themselves, eager to be independent. The care here is mostly positive, building strength both physically and mentally." She wished there was a way she could make him understand. "It's not perfect, obviously, but I like the fact that my patients rarely die. I like knowing they're on the final leg of their medical journey, ready to make new adjustments for the reward of going home."

He stared at her. "It's clear you love your job as much as I did."

She squared her jaw. He wasn't the only one who could be stubborn. "Yes, I do. But your career isn't over, Nick. Maybe you can't operate anymore, but there is so much good you can do. Look at all the wonderful things you've done as a hospitalist up here. I think the reason you're so good at this is because you understand, more than anyone, the impact of traumatic injuries."

He was silent for so long she thought he was simply going to turn and walk away but then he finally spoke in a low voice. "So you think physical medicine is the perfect choice for a cripple like me? No thanks. I'm a surgeon and I'm not ready to give up. Excuse me, I have work to do."

She couldn't think of a way to stop him from walking away. Even worse, she knew Nick wasn't just running from her, he was running from himself.

And she didn't know how to help him face the truth.

———————

NICK MANAGED to avoid Amber during the next few days. She'd had a shift off and even on the days she was working, he didn't stop to chat but concentrated on finishing his rounds.

Over the past ten days, he had noticed Roland's slacking off on his rounds. He'd set up a meeting with Rick Johnson the day before to discuss his concerns and was satisfied that the chief of staff would be issuing Roland a warning—either see his patients on a regular basis or risk having his admitting privileges revoked.

He hoped, for the patient's sake, that Roland would pull himself together and do the right thing. Practice medicine the way he should.

Nick hadn't seen Amber since earlier that morning. Now, as the hour was close to four o'clock in the afternoon, he assumed she'd already gone home. He should have been relieved, but part of him had wanted to see her once more.

He made his way downstairs, leaving the rehab unit. Last night he'd decided his temporary job here was finished. He'd packed his duffel bag earlier that morning and requested a late checkout from his room at The Cozy Inn. The only thing he had left to do was to get in touch with Johnson personally to let him know, with apologies for the short notice, that he was leaving.

Not just the hospital, but Milwaukee. He'd booked a 9:00 PM flight. Without a real place to call home, Nick figured he'd returned to Virginia, and to the hospital where he'd worked before leaving for Beijing.

He'd finish his physical therapy, and then what? He had

no idea. If he couldn't be a surgeon, he wasn't sure what he'd do.

He toyed with the idea of calling Amber to let her know he was leaving, but resisted the urge. She was the one person with the power to make him forget his plan, to turn him inside out. She'd gotten far too close, more so than any other woman he'd ever known. He knew if she asked him to stay longer, he would be tempted.

Even though he had nothing to offer her.

He thought for a moment about Shane. If Shane had lived, he would have asked Amber out upon returning home. Shane and Amber would have developed a relationship. Maybe one that would even have led to marriage. A family. Kids with cute names starting with the letter C to carry on the Monroe family tradition.

What did he know about relationships? Nothing. And he needed to figure out his own life before inflicting himself on a woman.

He walked outside, squinting in the bright sunlight. He began to cross the employee parking lot when he heard raised, heated voices.

"Do you have any idea what you've done to me, you little witch?"

"I didn't do anything to you, Dr. Roland. You did this completely on your own." Amber's voice, steady and firm, reached his ears.

"You ruined my career."

"Stop it! Let me go!"

Nick's eyes finally adjusted to the bright sunlight and for an awful moment he had a clear picture of Amber struggling with Roland near a fancy royal blue convertible.

He quickened his pace, limping and leaning on his cane. Before he could close the distance between them he saw Roland tighten his grip on Amber's shoulders and shake her, hard.

She cried out in alarm, shoving against his chest. "Stop it! You're hurting me."

"Let her go," Nick said sharply. Roland glanced his way. Amber took advantage of the moment, grinding one heel against his instep at the same time yanking free from his bruising grip.

Roland cursed and scowled when Amber broke free. He lunged for her, but she anticipated his move and side-stepped him. His fist managed to catch the fabric of her scrubs just enough that he yanked her toward him with surprising force.

This time Amber fought with what seemed to be wild desperation. He pushed himself to move faster, but the scene continued to unfold before him in slow motion.

"Let me go!" Her face grew red as she struggled against Roland's grip. Knocked off balance, they both fell against the sports car, with Amber pinned beneath Roland's bulk.

Nick grabbed the back of Roland's shirt and hauled him upright, yanking him away from Amber. "Stop it! What is your problem?"

Nick caught the odor of alcohol and knew.

Drunk. Roland was drunk. Maybe not staggering, stupid drunk. But he was definitely under the influence.

Roland ignored Nick, his attention still focused on Amber, and he glared at her where she leaned against the car. "What do you have against me? What did I ever do to you?"

"You've crossed the line, Roland." He didn't let go of him, worried he'd lunge toward Amber again. "You stay away from her, do you hear me?"

"It's all her fault. Everything is all her fault." Roland

continued to babble, but Nick sensed the worst of the danger was over. "She's trying to ruin me."

He shoved Roland aside with disgust. "As Amber said, you did that all by yourself."

The man slumped against the car as Nick crossed over to Amber. He drew her upright, pressing her against his lean frame. The dazed, horrified expression in her eyes tore at him. "Are you okay?"

"Yes." Her hands were shaking, and she reached down to massage her knee. She must have smacked it hard on the car when they'd fallen against it.

Nick barely glanced at Roland as he dug his cell phone out of his lab coat. "You'd better file formal assault charges this time. I'm sure this entire interaction was caught on the hospital security system. And if you don't call 911, I will."

CHAPTER TEN

"Don't be ridiculous". Amber straightened then shocked him by snatching the phone from his hand, quickly disconnecting the call. "You can't call 911 for this. It's not an emergency."

"You're hurt. That's enough of an emergency for me." Furious at Roland for laying a hand on her, he rounded on him, wrapping a fist in the front of the older man's shirt and pulling him close. "I'm telling you one last time. You had better stay away from her."

"Nick." She laid a hand on his arm. "I'm fine. Just let it go."

"I can't." Those endless moments before he could reach her would haunt him for a long time. "He threatened you."

"Threatened her? That's bull. I just wanted to talk to her." Rolland leaned backward, trying to break his hold. Apparently, Roland wasn't willing to pick on someone his own size. "I didn't mean to hurt her."

"Oh yeah? Maybe you should have thought of that before you grabbed her and shook her like a rag doll." She continued to pull on his arm, and with reluctance he let go of Roland's shirt. Taking a step back, he breathed deeply, struggling for control. "Get out of here, Roland. And don't even think about getting behind the wheel of your little blue convertible in your condition because I'll call the police. Did I mention Amber's brother is a cop? Something you should have thought about before manhandling her." He took his cell phone back from Amber. "Go and call yourself a rideshare."

Roland stumbled away, muttering obscenities under his breath. Letting him walk away wasn't easy—adrenaline raced through his system, making him yearn to blow off some steam by following Roland inside, maybe even escorting the guy all the way to Johnson's office. He wrestled himself under control and turned toward Amber. "Let me see your knee."

She lifted one leg of her scrub pants as high as it would go. Her right knee was swollen and already starting to bruise.

"We need ice. I'll help you back to the hospital. We can get an ice pack inside."

"No." Her voice was flat. "Roland headed that way."

He understood her reluctance and glanced across the street to The Cozy Inn, where he had a room—at least until five o'clock. "We can get ice from the motel. Do you think you can make it that far?"

"Sure." She sounded confident enough but when she put weight on her knee, she winced. "Maybe."

"Here, lean on me, I'll lean on my cane," he joked, trying not to sound as frustrated as he felt. Why couldn't he have moved just a little faster, to prevent Roland from hurting her?

Why hadn't his muscles obeyed his commands? If he hadn't been hampered by his injuries, he could have stopped Roland and diffused the situation before things had gotten so far out of hand.

"Stop it." Amber must have been able to read his mind, because she jabbed him lightly in the ribs with her index finger. "You've got to stop taking responsibility for other people's actions. For their decisions. Roland hurt my knee—you didn't. Besides, I was stupid enough to try talking to him in the first place."

He raised a brow as they made their way across the street. "Did you smell the alcohol on his breath?"

She sighed. "Not until after I was too close. Then when I tried to back off, he grabbed me. He was so angry, nothing I said got through to him."

He wondered if her wrist was bruised as well and vowed to take a closer look once they were inside. They crossed the mostly vacant parking lot of the motel. He hesitated outside the door to his room. His packed duffle was standing just inside the door. Well, there wasn't anything he could do about it now. With a sinking feeling in the pit of his stomach, he unlocked the door and helped her in.

The muscles in her body stiffened the moment she caught sight of his bag.

"You're leaving?"

"Yeah."

"Tonight?"

He hid a wince and nodded.

"Without saying goodbye?" Her tone was incredulous.

He escorted Amber over to the bed, where she could sit and take the pressure off her knee. This was exactly what he tried to avoid. The wounded expression in her eyes sliced him like a scalpel.

"Sit down. I'll get you some ice." Once she was settled on the edge of the bed, he grabbed the ice bucket and a plastic bag, then headed out to the ice machine at the end of the row of rooms. Filling the bucket halfway only took a minute, and when he returned to his room, the wounded expression in her eyes was still there.

Awkwardly, ignoring the pain in his leg, he knelt before her and gently pressed the makeshift cold pack on the swollen part of her knee. Because she kept staring at him accusingly, he felt compelled to respond.

"Amber, not long ago I discovered you were moving to Florida without mentioning that to me. And today you're upset because I was going to leave without saying good-bye?" He ran his gaze over her ivory cheeks, noting how her freckles stood out in sharp contrast to her pale skin. "We don't want the same things. I never intended to hurt you." He hid a wince at how that sounded just like Roland.

"So where are you going?" She stared at his duffel, placed neatly against the wall by the door. Slowly she brought her gaze to his. "I know you're going home, but where is home? In Chicago?"

Chicago? Where had she gotten that idea? Then he remembered telling her he'd grown up there, that they were practically neighbors. There wasn't any specific place he ever thought of as home. It was on the tip of his tongue to admit the truth, but then he caught himself just in time. "No, not Chicago. I have a condo across from the Fairfax hospital in Virginia.

"Oh, I see. It sounds nice."

Nice? His condo wasn't nice. It was empty. Lonely. And about as impersonal as this motel room. He'd bought it furnished a year or so ago it would have been ashamed to show her the place. He didn't have any personal belongings there. No books, no art, no family pictures.

Other than his clothes, there was nothing in the place that he'd personally purchased.

His so-called home was as far from the noisy, crowded Monroe household, with its comfortable eclectic furniture and wall of framed photographs as you could get.

Before he could gather his thoughts, she pushed his hand holding the ice on her knee. "It's too cold," she protested. "I'm fine."

Dark smudges encircling her wrist caught his gaze, and he set the ice aside and took her hand in his. "Look at what that jerk did to you."

"I'm fine," she repeated in a stubborn tone. But he didn't believe her. The tremor in her fingers ripped at his heart. And what would Roland have done if he hadn't gotten there in time? Would that jerk have gone as far as to sexually assault her. The thought made him burn with a fresh wave of anger.

Before he could talk himself out of it, he bent and placed a quick kiss on the bruises marring her wrist. "I'm so sorry. I'm here for you."

There was a long moment of silence, before she spoke. "For a minute, when I was pinned underneath him, I couldn't breathe..." She didn't finish.

"I know." He reached up and smoothed a hand over her hair. "I wish I could have gotten to you sooner."

She shook her head. Her lack of feistiness bothered him more than he wanted to admit. He stood, ignoring the jolt of pain in his leg, then settled beside her on the edge of the bed. The mattress dipped, bringing her body closer to his. He wrapped his arm around her shoulders and pulled her against him.

To his shocked surprise she slid one arm around his

waist and turned into his embrace, tucking her face into the curve of his shoulder.

He wanted to erase the awful memories from her mind. With a quick motion he lifted her knees and turned her so she was sitting on his lap. Tense, he waited for her to break out of his embrace, but she didn't. Instead, she held on tight.

He didn't know how long he held her, only that he withstood the pain in his leg for as long as possible, before shifting her weight to the other side.

She muttered a soft moan, but didn't stir.

With a wry smile, he realized she must have fallen asleep. He wasn't sure if he should be irritated, or flattered.

Careful not to wake her, he slid backwards until they were both stretched out in the bed. He drew one end of the bedspread over her, then tucked her against his chest. With his chin nestled in her hair, he relaxed against the pillow.

If all he could do for her was to give her an hour of peaceful sleep, then that's what he would do. Although holding her in his arms like this, mere hours before he was scheduled to leave, was sweet, sweet torture.

A FIERCE BANGING woke Amber from a sound sleep. Confused, she lifted her head and glanced around.

"Open up, Tanner! I know you're in there." The words were emphasized by more pounding.

"Stop it, I'm coming." She crawled from the bed, straightening her scrubs as she did. Nick stirred on the bed. The room was dark, indicating she and Nick must have slept for hours. Nothing inappropriate had happened, however she suspected her family thought the worst.

"Amber? Open this door or I'll break it in!"

Knowing her brother wasn't kidding, she flicked on the light and wrenched the door open. "Alec, what is your problem?"

"What are you guys doing?" Dressed in full cop gear, Alec shouldered past her, scanning the room like a madman. Thank goodness she and Nick were dressed and that nothing had happened. Not that Nick would ever cross the line like that. And neither would she. "Do you realize we just busted a drug deal in a room on the second floor of this motel?"

"A drug deal?" She stared at him. "What does that have to do with me? With us?" She shut the door, trying hard not to slam it. Nick had risen to his feet and stood on the opposite side of the double bed, watching her brother with a wary eye. "You're acting crazy, busting in here like a madman."

"Why didn't you answer your phone?" Alec didn't give an inch, standing with a wide stance as if he was ready to go for his gun at any second.

With a guilty flush, she glanced around for her purse. She'd left it on the floor near the bed. Picking it up, she found her cell phone that she'd left on vibrate. She always kept it on vibrate while working. She winced when she saw there were nine missed calls.

She tossed the phone back in her purse. "I was busy." Alec wouldn't be acting this way if it was her brother Adam here in a motel room.

"Too busy to consider Mom's needs?" Alec's accusing glance swept over the wrinkled bed into her equally wrinkled clothes.

Guilt burned the back of her throat like lye. "I'm sorry. I know I should have called, but I am not the only child she has. And that's no excuse for your behavior,

Alec. We didn't do anything wrong. You're wired a little too tight."

Nick found his voice. "But now that he's here, tell him what happened with Roland. I know you're more upset than you let on."

Alec's gaze narrowed, bouncing between the two of them. "What do you mean? What happened?"

Great, just what she needed—more fuel to pour on her brother's fiery temper. She shot Nick a narrowed look, warning him to keep his mouth shut. "Nothing. Never mind."

"What happened?" Ignoring her, Alec addressed Nick.

"The medical director of the unit that Amber works for was drunk, grabbed her shoulders and shook her hard enough to make her teeth rattle. Then when she tried to escape, he grabbed her again then fell on her, pinning her against the car." Nick waved at her. "Trust me, she has the bruises to prove it."

Alec spun toward her.

"Forget it." She crossed her arms and resisted the urge to scream at the top of her lungs. What was it about her brothers that made them deaf and dumb when it came to her wishes? "You come storming in here like some psycho and now you want to talk rationally? Get out Alec. I am twenty-six years old. I don't need you to watch over me." A strangled laugh bubbled out through her tight throat. "This is exactly why I can't wait to move to Florida. After this stunt of yours, I may not even bother to give you my address once I'm settled."

Her brother clenched his jaw. "We care about you, Amber. No one was able to reach you for hours. That gives us a right to be worried. Let me see your bruises, who is this guy? We can still pick him up for assault."

"You are not arresting anyone." She glanced at her watch and winced at the late hour. "It's ten o'clock at night. Don't you have real bad guys to catch? Go chase your drug dealers and leave me alone."

Alec stared at her for a long minute, as if reassuring himself she was really alright. Then he moved toward the door. "Mom and Dad have been frantic, wondering what happened to you. You better call them."

"I will." She stood her ground.

Alec glanced at Nick's bag propped beside the door. He raised a brow. "Leaving?"

Nick shrugged. "Eventually. Why?"

"Just wondering." Alec's smile seemed laced with satisfaction. "See you later, Amber."

"Not if I see you, first." She gave her brother a shove, surprising him enough to make him stumble. "Goodbye Alec."

When the door closed behind her brother, she dropped onto the edge of the bed and cradled her head in her hands. Her voice was muffled. "I'm sorry."

"Why? Because you have a family who cares about you?" Nick limped over to pick up his cane.

"No. because they're certifiably crazy." With a deep sigh, she lifted her head. "Especially my brothers. Alec is much worse since he became a cop. You can see why I'm so desperate to get away from them."

"Yeah, well, I'm afraid I don't really get that. It's nice to have someone who cares about you. And I still think you should have told your brother about Roland without my prompting. He deserves to be punished for what he did to you." He stepped around the bed, and almost fell, catching himself in time.

She frowned. Had Nick re-injured his leg? He'd

continued to work out in the physical therapy gym each day on top of his hospitalist work. She suspected he'd cut way back on his pain medication, too. The incident with Roland probably hadn't helped.

She tensed and shivered. There was no denying she seriously feared for her safety when Roland had pressed her against the car. She'd half expected him to grab her breasts, or worse. Maybe Nick was right. But if she did decide to press charges, her brother would be the last person she'd go to.

She drew in a calming breath. "I meant to thank you for coming to my rescue."

"It was dumb luck that I happened to be there."

She didn't agree. She felt certain God had sent him to her as a way to protect her from Roland, and to prevent him from leaving without saying goodbye. But she wasn't sure if Nick wanted to hear that. "Do you think Roland has a drinking problem? Maybe his drinking is the reason he hasn't been making rounds?"

"I don't know." Nick pursed his lips." I assumed Johnson had given him an ultimatum about getting his act together, and that caused Roland to head out for a few drinks." He raised a brow. "Unless you think he's been under the influence before?"

"Hmm. I don't know." She wrinkled her brow, thinking back to their extremely brief conversations. "Not that I can say for sure. There was one time I thought he slurred his words, but then he seemed fine."

"It's a big leap from one or two episodes of drinking too much to a full-fledged alcohol problem that could interfere with his work."

She didn't necessarily agree. "Come on, Nick, how could we know? He's hardly ever around to smell the alcohol on him. What do we really know about his mental state while he's given orders to us from the other end of a phone?"

"You have a point," he agreed. He crossed the room, but didn't come close enough to touch her.

She wished, more than anything, she could have woken up in his arms. To have kissed him, the way she'd longed to.

Nick stared at her, a frowned furrowing his brow. "I don't know where to go from here."

She swallowed hard and tried to sound casual, although her heart was thumping in her chest. "Why? Because you missed your flight?"

"Partially." He shrugged then turned away. "I guess this means I'm not leaving after all."

"You're not?" Hope swelled at his words. Even after her brother's rudeness, Nick was staying.

Nick was staying!

"No, I'm not leaving until I know exactly what is going on with Roland."

She wanted to tell him how glad she was that he wasn't leaving yet but didn't want him to take her comment the wrong way. He didn't say he was staying for her, so there was no reason to plan an entire future with him. But he seemed to care about her.

"You really think he could have a drinking problem?"

He nodded. "Yeah. Now that you've put the idea in my head, I can't leave until I know for sure that Roland isn't practicing under the influence. Because if he is, he either needs to sign himself into a treatment program or have his license suspended until he agrees to go."

"Okay, then. Sounds like a plan." She smoothed her hand over her wrinkled scrubs. "I'd better head home."

"I'll walk you home."

She moved toward the door, hoping Roland would get the help he needed. And Nick staying in Milwaukee would give her time to make a few phone calls. There was no reason she had to go all the way to Florida to get away from her family.

Virginia would work just as well.

CHAPTER ELEVEN

As Nick walked her home, the idea of moving to Virginia grew, expanding in her chest. Amber knew the nursing shortage was prevalent everywhere, there must be traveling nurse assignments in Virginia, too. There were still a couple of weeks before she was scheduled to leave. Easy enough to call the travel nurse agency and request a switch in her assignment. Hopefully, they wouldn't mind.

Thrilled with the idea, she felt as if she were walking on air. The distance between Nick's motel and home was almost too short. They reached her parents' house in record time.

He stopped at the foot of the stairs leading to the wide wrap around porch. "Goodnight, Amber." He hadn't taken her hand, although she wished he had.

"Good night." When he turned as if to walk away, she leaned up to kiss him. This time he didn't duck fast enough. Her intention had been to keep things light, but in a heart-beat his mouth fused with hers.

He pulled her close. She reveled in the warmth of his embrace.

Then he broke off the kiss, breathing heavily. "The taste of you goes straight to my head."

It was the nicest thing any man had ever said to her. "And that's a bad thing?"

"Yeah." He cleared his throat and took another step back. "I better go, before one of your brothers shows up."

Irritation flashed, darkened lethal. "They don't run my life, no matter what they think. I'm moving out of here as soon as possible."

"Easy." He held up a hand. "I was only teasing. I think it's sweet the way they look out for you."

"It's not sweet. It's annoying." Her buoyant mood had been shattered by her family's interference once again. With a sigh she rubbed her forehead. "Never mind. Will I see you tomorrow?"

"Sure. I'll call you." He flashed a warm smile, then turned and headed back down the street the way they'd come.

She stayed where she was, not quite ready to go inside. Thankfully the house was quiet, her parents were sleeping peacefully, despite Alec's attempt to make her feel guilty. She couldn't believe Nick hadn't been angry at her brother's irrational behavior. The nerve of him, barging into Nick's motel room to find her, playing on her mother's concern. Which was totally ridiculous. Other than needing a little help moving around, her mother was doing fine.

In fact, her mom was doing so well, there was no reason to wait until the middle of August to leave.

Maybe she should put in her notice first thing Monday morning. Waiting the entire weekend would be hard, but at least she could spend some time with Nick.

Remembering his sizzling kiss made it difficult to fall asleep.

NICK WALKED to the physical therapy gym first thing the next morning. The manager of The Cozy Inn had been more than happy for Nick to extend his visit a few more days, especially after the bad press related to the drug bust. At least Alec hadn't been lying about that. He considered relocating to a different motel, but the manager had given him a discount to stay.

As much as he'd wanted to leave, to get far away from the temptation of spending time with Amber, he couldn't go without uncovering the truth about Roland.

Was she right? Did Roland have a drinking problem? He sincerely hoped not. Although he hated to admit, it would explain the guy's behavior. Especially the way he'd assaulted Amber.

Once he finished his physical therapy session, he planned to wander up to the rehab unit. He wasn't required to see patients on the weekends, unless on call. Which he wasn't, at least not this weekend. But since he'd never gotten in touch with Johnson about his intent to leave, he had every right to be up on the unit.

While working in the gym, Nick had strained his muscles to the limit on the weight machines, even though he suspected his efforts were in vain. Pumping all the iron in the world wasn't going to replace the damaged nerves in his hand to the point he could go back to being a surgeon.

Walking without the help of a cane was still a good motivator, though, so he concentrated on working his legs, lifting weights until his muscles screamed and trembled with agony. He pushed himself as hard as he dared, before stopping.

After a long, hot shower, he put on his lab coat over his

casual clothes and headed up to the second floor rehab unit. When he walked on the floor, the first thing he saw was a brand new patient lying in the hallway, waiting for the cleaning crew to finish in the room.

The kid was young, couldn't have been more than twenty-two or twenty-three years old. Nick found himself wondering what had happened to bring him to the hospital when he noticed the lack of a bump under the covers where his right leg should have been.

His heart took a nosedive. The young soldier had lost his leg.

He found himself massaging his own injured thigh, and quickly dropped his hand. He stepped forward and nodded at the patient. "I'm Dr. Tanner. How are you?"

"Fine." The kids monotone voice and the way he stared at the ceiling over his head convinced Nick he was anything but fine. He hesitated for a moment, torn by indecision, then continued on his way to the nurse's station.

"What's the name of our new patient?" He asked.

"Hmm. You must mean Billy Anderson." The nurses name tag red Margaret, and she gestured toward the computer screen in front of her. "I'm getting him admitted into the system right now. He came from the ortho unit."

"Thanks." Moving to another vacant computer desk, he took a moment to log in and check Billy Anderson's medical record. The kid's diagnosis jumped out at him. Right leg amputation as the result of an IED explosion. He clenched his jaw, imagining what the kid had suffered.

Amber was wrong, working rehab wasn't his expertise at all. The last thing he wanted was to talk to Billy Anderson, who had every right to be angry at the world.

He knew just how the kid felt.

Glancing over his shoulder, he watched as a nurse's aide

pushed Billy's bed into the newly cleaned room. The kid continued to stare at the ceiling, acting as if he couldn't care less where they stuck him. The expression of tense hopelessness struck a resonant chord.

He continued scanning the young man's past medical history and current level of care. A few minutes later, he scrubbed his hands over his face. Billy's story was similar in many ways to his own. The main difference was that Nick had chosen to charter a plane so they could fly over the Great Wall of China. Billy had been simply doing his job as a soldier. And now, he had lost his leg because of his determination to serve his country.

He forced himself to stand. According to the medical record, Roland had already completed an initial assessment on Billy. It struck him as odd, though, because normally assessments were done once the patient was in a room. Maybe after being chastised by Johnson, Roland had actually gone to the orthopedic unit to complete the assessment.

"Which nurse is taking care of the new patient, Billy Anderson," he asked.

Betty, the unit coordinator glanced up. "Margaret, she's in the room with him now."

"Has Roland been in here recently?"

She nodded. "Yes, but he didn't stay long. Just mentioned something about completing the assessment and the new transfer, then he left. Billy Anderson is the only new patient we're scheduled to receive today."

A cowardly relief swept through him. At least he wouldn't have to go in to do the assessment himself. As a young otherwise healthy twenty-three-year-old, there was no need for Nick to examine him as a hospitalist on the unit. His role was to monitor the medical needs of the patients who had other medical concerns. He was to assist in treating hypertension, chronic obstructive pulmonary disease, and other medical co-morbidities. Roland was responsible for the rehab component of the patient's care.

"Thanks for letting me know." He paused, then asked, "Did Roland seem okay?"

Betty shrugged. "He was the same as usual, rude and short tempered." She reached for the ringing phone.

There was no way he could ask if she'd smelled alcohol and Roland's breath—those sorts of questions would only result in the spread of nasty rumors. As much as he didn't care for the guy, especially after the scene he'd witnessed with him assaulting Amber, encouraging speculation wouldn't be fair. In this instance, Roland was innocent of being an alcoholic, until proven guilty.

He turned and headed down the hall to double check on those patients who did need his expertise, even though he wasn't required to work weekends, he may as well do a quick review. When he deemed everything was under control, he turned and left the unit.

Roland probably didn't have a drinking problem at all. Nick grimaced, realizing he'd made the decision to stay in Milwaukee for nothing. In fact, Roland seemed to be on top of things this morning. Going to Dr. Johnson with his concerns had probably been the kick in the pants Roland had needed to get his act together.

Outside, the hot summer sun beat down on his head. Last night he'd promised to call Amber, but now he hesitated. As much as he wanted to be with her, he knew better than to give in to temptation.

Guilt hit hard at how they'd fallen asleep. Innocently enough, but he could tell Alec had believed otherwise. And honestly, if the situation had been reversed, he'd have assumed the worst, too. He didn't blame her brother for being concerned.

Amber was young, innocent and had her whole life ahead of her. She wanted to travel, to experience life at its fullest, and she deserved to do exactly that. His hand tightened on his cane. What could he offer? Especially now, when he was at a crossroads. He needed a place to settle down. A place to start over.

A place to find himself.

"Nick?" Hearing Amber's voice made him frown. Had thinking of her conjured the sound? "I've been looking for you."

Dressed in a pair of denim shorts, and a blue top that matched her eyes, she looked adorable. He felt the tightness in his chest ease. Gazing at her made him feel young. Healthy. Ready to take on the world.

For a moment, Billy's blank stare invaded his mind. He shoved it away. He couldn't help the kid feel better. Not when he could barely help himself.

He cleared his throat. "I went to the PT gym to do some physical therapy, then checked things out up on the rehab unit." He smiled when she approached. "You'll be glad to know Roland was in earlier this morning, actually making rounds."

"No way!" Her eyes widened. "I don't believe it."

"It's true." He held up a hand. "Scouts honor."

"You were a Scout?" Skepticism laced her tone. "Somehow, I have trouble picturing you wearing a Boy Scout uniform sporting all those badges of accomplishments."

He chuckled. "All right, you win. I was never a boy scout. But I wasn't lying about Roland. Betty saw him making rounds."

"I'm glad. It's about time he took his responsibilities seriously." She shook her head. "I wouldn't care if it wasn't the patients who suffer as a result of his lack of attentiveness."

"I agree."

"Are you finished for the day? Because if so, let's go."

"Go where?"

"To German Fest, silly." She raked a critical gaze over his casual slacks and button down shirt. "You'll be too hot dressed like that. I'll wait while you change."

He doubted German Fest was anything like actually being in Germany, where he'd been stationed. It made him smile to think that the Milwaukee version would consist of beer guzzling men shouting, "Gemutliechkeit!"

What did it matter? It would be better than sitting inside his motel room. The logical side of his head told him to decline her offer, to stay far away from her until it was time to book himself another flight back to Virginia.

Instead, he heard himself answer, "Sure. I'll be right back."

AMBER SNEAKED several glances at Nick as they walked through the lakefront festival grounds. She'd borrowed Alec's car since he was working again, and there had been no sign of the rental Nick had gotten for their date at DiCarlos's restaurant. She'd pointed out to her brother that he owed her a favor after barging into Nick's motel room, and he'd reluctantly agreed. It didn't come close to payback for his rude behavior, but it was a start.

The ride downtown was unusually quiet. She was getting the distinct impression Nick wouldn't have called if she hadn't gone looking for him.

Uncertainty gnawed at her. Was she pushing too hard? Yeah, probably. It wasn't like her to chase after a guy. Or maybe it was, since she'd longed for something more with Shane, too.

The thought brought her up short. Maybe this wasn't a good idea. Then again, spending a few hours at the festival would be fun. And Nick seemed as if he could use the outing.

Friendship, she silently reminded herself. This day would be about friendship.

"That looks good," Nick said, eyeing two men walking by with huge bratwursts slathered with sauerkraut.

"Usinger's famous sausage, my favorite." Her mouth watered at the pungent scent. "I'm sure it's not the same as what you'd get in Germany, but it still tastes great. Come on, let's grab lunch."

"I'm game." He insisted on paying for their two sausages, then led the way to an empty spot at a picnic table. "I have to admit, it looks exactly like the food we had in Germany."

"Really?" She was glad to hear it. She grinned and took a big bite. "Maybe I'll get to Germany, one day. At least I know the food is good."

He chuckled and took a bite of his own meal. "This is great."

When they finished eating, she led the way to one of the stages where a band and dancers were assembled. The bright blue and green costumes flared when one of the girls twirled experimentally. "Okay, I know this probably isn't as authentic as being in Germany, but it's still awesome to watch."

"The whole festival is far more realistic than I would have imagined." He nodded at the stage. "How many different bands play here?"

"About a dozen." She grinned. "During Summer Fest

there are far more bands playing, every music genre you can imagine. But for the ethnic festivals, they stick with the music favored by that country."

"Wow." He looked around in surprise. "Do you have festivals like this all summer?"

"Yep, starting in June and going into September. Festa Italiana, Irish Fest, Polish Fest, Mexican Fiesta." She ticked them off on her fingers. "Those are my favorites. There are more, but I can't honestly say I've been to them all."

They wandered around the grounds, listening to the variety of folk music and trying different types of German food.

"I think the Schnitzel was my favorite," Nick admitted, licking his fingers after eating the tasty treat. "And don't tell anyone, but I think this one tasted better than what I had when stationed in Germany."

She laughed. "I won't."

They sat and watched a variety of shows, people watching, as much as enjoying the entertainment. Oddly the time seemed to fly by. They ate dinner at another of the German restaurant tents, until Nick protested that he couldn't eat another bite.

Later that evening, as dusk fell, they made their way closer to the lakefront.

"We need to find a good spot." She scanned the grassy area intently. Several yards away, she noticed a perfect area partially hidden by an outcropping of rocks.

"For what?" He raised a brow.

"To watch the drone show. They've replaced fireworks here with drones, because of the fire hazard." She tugged on his arm. "Let's head this way, where there are less people."

"We are going to get eaten alive by mosquitoes."

She glanced at him over her shoulder, as she led the way

on a zigzag path through the other onlookers. "Don't worry. Once we've claimed our squatter's rights, I'll go back to Alec's car and get a blanket and can of bug spray." She grinned. "Come on, did you really think I was a rookie at this?"

"Guess not."

Once she'd gotten Nick settled in the spot where she wanted to sit, she headed back to her brother's car. The night air was still warm, so there was no need for a sweatshirt. She did grab Alec's oversized blanket and mosquito spray. She walked back to where she'd left Nick, smiling at the way he was stretched out on his side, his head propped on his elbow, looking as relaxed as she'd ever seen him.

"I'm glad you took your pain medicine today," she said.

He rolled up to his feet, grimacing a bit. "Nope, I didn't take any pain meds today." He held out his hand so she gave him one end of the blanket. Together they spread it on the ground. Then they both took a seat. Her shoulder brushed his as she curled her arms around her bent knees.

"Beautiful," Nick murmured. She glanced over expecting him to be looking out at Lake Michigan. But his gaze was centered on her.

She almost leaned over to kiss him again. But then the flash of light caught her eye. The drone show was about to start.

How they managed to get the drones to make designs in the sky was a mystery. She caught her breath as purple and green drones lifted to the sky, making a large mushroom.

"Wow." Nick gazed upward a smile tugging at the corner of his mouth. "I like this. It's quiet, but still stunning. Better for those veterans who can't tolerate the sound of fireworks because it reminds them of gunfire."

"I agree." She had taken care of many of those patients, herself. "This is a really nice alternative."

The drones winked out. Then turned back on, bright red and white sparkles blooming in the sky. Followed quickly by blue drones shooting through the red and white ones. She couldn't take her gaze off the show, as the drones made different pictures in the sky.

The grand finale was a large American flag shining in the sky for long moments. When the drones winked out, the audience whistled and applauded.

"I've never seen a drone show before," Nick said, his voice low and husky near her ear. "Thanks for bringing me here."

"Any time," she murmured. Sending him a sideways glance, she found he was close. Close enough to kiss. But she had initiated their last kiss, so she didn't attempt to close the gap between them.

Yet she was keenly aware of him sitting close beside her. The other men in her life paled in comparison to Nick. Even Shane.

Especially Shane.

Looking back now, she realized that despite her wanting more, her feelings for Shane had been that of a close friendship. The sizzling awareness that hovered between her and Nick was something she'd never experienced before. It seemed so obvious now, that if Shane had lived, there never would have been anything serious between them. She still missed Shane, but it was more of an ache than a deep stabbing pain.

"How long can we hang out here?" Nick asked.

"As long as we want to, I guess." She smiled. "I don't mind sitting around for a while. The way people are streaming out of here, we'll be alone, soon."

"Not sure that's a good idea," he muttered half under his breath.

"Because you don't want to?" She couldn't help wondering why he was holding back. She'd made her interest in him pretty clear.

Hadn't she?

His gaze pierced hers. "No because I want to kiss you again."

Her heart thundered against her sternum. "I'm not stopping you."

"You should." When she didn't move, or say anything, he wrapped his arm around her shoulders and pulled her close. He lowered his head and captured her lips with his. This time, there was no one around to interrupt their embrace.

When they finally needed to breathe, Nick rested his cheek on the top of her hair. "I hate to say this, but I think we should go."

"I guess." There was no enthusiasm in her tone. She wasn't ready for the evening to end.

"I expect your brother Alec to show up at any moment," Nick said in a wry tone.

"Oh please. I have his car, so that's not likely." She huffed. "I'm glad for the chance to escape my family, at least for a while."

"Like all day?" he asked.

She sighed, then reached for her purse to check her phone. "Oops. Guess I left my cell phone off."

"Didn't you do that last night, as well?" Nick shook his head. "I think they're onto your tricks."

"I wouldn't have to play tricks, if my nosy siblings would just leave me alone." She turned her phone on, not surprised to see there were at least four messages. She sighed. Her family never gave up.

She was tempted to ignore them, unwilling to give up this private time with Nick. But then frowned, realizing most of the messages were from her sister, Andrea. Not her brothers. Or her parents. But Andrea. Her older sister was the one sibling who didn't normally bother her too much.

"That's strange."

"What's wrong?" Nick asked with a frown.

"I'm not sure." She clicked the voicemail button, to listen to the most recent message.

"Bethany was hit by a car. They took her to Children's Memorial Hospital." Her sister's sobbing voice echoed in the night. "Where are you? Please, call me. I need you."

"Oh no!" Horrified, she jumped to her feet. "Hurry. My niece Beth was hit by a car. I need to go see her!"

CHAPTER TWELVE

Nick knew how upset Amber had been after finding out Mr. Goetz had died, but this situation hit far closer to home. He insisted on driving her to the hospital, and it was a testimony as to how distraught she was that she didn't argue. As he drove, she tried to call her sister back, but Andrea didn't answer. Frantic, she listened to her phone messages while he negotiated traffic.

"Any more information?" He glanced at her when she lowered the phone to her lap.

"No." She clamped her lowered lip between her teeth. "I should never have turned my phone off. It was a foolishly, irresponsible thing to do. My sister sounded so upset. Poor Beth. Oh, Nick, what if she's really hurt? I can't stand it. Please, hurry."

"Don't think the worst." He pushed the speed limit as much as he dared. "I'm sure she's going to be fine."

"You don't know that." She turned to stare out the window, her jaw tight. "She's only six years old. A baby—" her voice broke.

He captured her hand in his, holding tight. He didn't

know what to say, so he fell silent. For all Amber's tough talk about moving away, she was still very close to her family. How would she cope if this had happened while she'd been in Florida? He couldn't imagine.

He'd seen a variety of outcomes for children struck by cars. Many factors came into play in determining the outcome. Had the child been hit while walking? Or riding a bike? Had she been wearing a helmet? Had the car only clipped her or hit directly head on?

As part of his trauma training, he'd done a stint at a children's hospital in Baltimore. The number of kids hit by cars while riding their bikes was astronomical. The worst injuries were caused by kids not wearing helmets. If Beth had been on a bike, he silently prayed she'd been wearing some type of head protection.

He pulled into the parking lot at Children's Memorial and circled around to the emergency entrance. He'd barely stopped the car when she shot out of her seat and raced inside.

He parked in the closest empty spot, then slid out from behind the wheel. He grabbed his cane, following at a slower pace, feeling guilty for the role he'd played in keeping her out of touch with her family. He'd been selfishly enjoying their time together, especially kissing her, when he knew a relationship between them would be impossible.

The Monroe family took up at least half of the waiting room. As Nick approached, he noticed Amber's brother, Adam, the pediatric doc wasn't there. His gaze landed on Andrea. She was in the middle of the group, holding on to her toddler son and rocking back and forth, looking as if she was in shock.

No surprise there.

Amber knelt beside her sister and engulfed her in a hug. Nick stopped just outside the family circle, knowing he didn't belong here, yet straining to overhear the conversation.

"What happened? How is she? What are they doing for her?" Amber fired questions faster than an army drill Sergeant.

"She has a compound fracture in her right leg, they're talking about taking her to surgery." Andrea sniffled and swiped at her eyes. "She was riding her bike in the drive-way, I always tell her not to go into the road, but she must have gone out to make a wide turn. Mr. Henderson, the neighbor across the street, was backing out of his driveway and didn't see her. Thankfully, he wasn't going very fast."

"And Beth was wearing her helmet, right?" Amber bent and brushed a kiss across Ben's forehead.

"Yes." Andrea's voice was faint, rough along the edges from crying. "We've been here in the emergency depart-ment for hours, they're short on beds up on the ortho floor. Adam is in there with her now while they prepare her for surgery. Ben was crying and wouldn't calm down so Dad came in to get me."

"I'll sit here with Ben you go back in to be with your daughter." Amber's tone was firm and she gently lifted the little boy from her sister's lap and hugged him close. Nick expected the toddler to protest but he didn't seem to mind.

"Thanks." Andrea stood and quickly left the waiting room. Nick felt like a third wheel, he wasn't part of this family, no matter how welcome they'd made him feel when inviting him to dinner.

Before he could move, Alec stepped up beside him. "Thanks for bringing Amber. We were worried when she didn't answer her phone."

Nick swallowed a sigh. He wasn't at the phone police, yet he wished she hadn't shut it off. He could understand their concern. "We were at German Fest. We ate food, hung out for a while, then watched the drone show."

Alex stared at him grimly. "And what, the drone show was so loud she couldn't hear her phone over the noise?"

"She had her phone off." Nick wasn't about to lie. "Look, I know she shouldn't have done that, but you guys are just a little overprotective." He shrugged. "I get it. And I don't even mind. I told Amber I thought it was nice the way you guys looked after her."

With the scowl Alec turned and glanced at his sister. "Being nice isn't the goal."

"Yeah, that's what she said, too. And therein lies the problem. Like I said, I understand both sides of this." He followed Alec's gaze, then sucked in a quick breath. Cuddling Ben close, Amber's face held nurturing expression. One that he could easily envision her bestowing on her own child. His child.

Their child.

Wait a minute, where had that thought sprung from?

He wasn't ready to have kids, not by a long shot. He couldn't even support himself. He swallowed hard and glanced away. He wasn't ready for children, or marriage for that matter. But if there ever came a time for him to want a child of his own, he couldn't imagine a better mother than Amber.

"I have to go." He dug the key fob from his pocket and handed it to Alec. "She borrowed your car, right? I'm sure you'll give Amber a ride home."

Alec stared at him for a moment. "How are you going to get back to your hotel?"

Nick shrugged. "I'll call a ride share."

"I'll drive you. I have a police cruiser parked outside." Alec leaned over to his father, who was sitting next to his wife. Nick couldn't hear what Alex said, but then he straightened, and turned toward the door. "Let's go."

He hesitated and glanced at Amber, but she was preoccupied with the child in her arms. She was knee deep in conversation with her family and he didn't think it was prudent to interrupt. He had no business being here. Clearly, this was a family matter. He turned and followed Alec outside.

Once they were settled in the cruiser, Alec said, "So, tell me more about this guy Roland." Alec turned down the sound of the volume of his police radio as he pulled out into traffic. "Where can I find him?"

"At the VA hospital." Nick raised a brow. "You can't do anything about Roland if Amber won't press charges."

"That may not be the case, depending on what he did to her." Alex sent him an enigmatic sidelong glance. "What happened?"

He explained the altercation he'd witnessed near Roland's sporty blue car. When he finished, Alec was scowling.

"I can't believe it!" Alec thumped a hand on the steering wheel. "Why in blazes wouldn't she press charges? The guy is a menace."

Considering how badly he'd wanted her to press charges, he knew exactly how her brother felt. Now, he wasn't so sure. Hadn't Roland come in that morning to make rounds? Maybe the guy was just going through a bad time. Based on Johnson's ultimatum, he felt sure Roland likely leave her alone now. Nick offered a wry grin. "I don't think you have to worry. I may have happened to mention how Amber's brother was a cop."

"Good." Alec didn't so much as crack a smile. "What's his first name? I'll run him through the system, see what pops."

"Douglas. But I doubt you'll find anything. All physicians have criminal background checks done on a regular basis. If there was something there, he wouldn't be in his current position."

"Still can't hurt to check." Alec pulled into the parking lot of The Cozy Inn. "Thanks again for being there for Amber."

"You're welcome." He was surprised Alec hadn't continued to grill him over what he and Amber had been doing down at the lakefront. Not that their heated kiss was any of her brother's business. So why did he feel guilty?

He pushed open the car door and swung his legs out. The muscle of his left leg spasmed badly. This was the price he'd paid by not taking any pain meds. It galled him to show his weakness in front of Amber's brother. Gripping the door with one hand and the frame overhead with the other he gritted his teeth and pulled himself upright.

Darkness blurred his vision and for a moment he slumped against the door. When he heard Alec's car door open, he gathered himself together with an effort.

"Need a hand?" Alec's previous hostility was gone. The guy watched him warily.

Embarrassment crawled up the back of his neck, settling on his shoulders like a living, breathing beast. "No."

In response, Alec pulled out his cane and handed it to him. He forced himself to take the stupid thing, and to slowly, painfully, make his way toward his room. Alec walked behind him, is if waiting for him to fall. Sheer grit and determination kept him moving forward until he could unlock his door and step across the threshold.

As he glanced back over his shoulder Alec gave him a nod then turned to climb back into his cruiser.

He should have appreciated the way Alec had looked after him, but instead his ego felt as if someone had dug into an open wound with sharp fingernails. Once inside his hotel room, he collapsed on the bed. The fiery pain in his leg throbbed, and he took several deep breaths in a vain attempt to control the sharp edges slicing through him.

Only when the pain receded to a tolerable level did he allow himself to think back to the day he'd spent with Amber. Sharing a meal, talking, laughing, sitting close in the darkness while watching the drone show. And kissing her.

His chest tightened and his eyes flew open in alarm as the realization hit.

He loved her.

He wasn't sure how it had happened, or why. He hadn't been looking for this. Yet somehow, he'd fallen in love with Amber Monroe.

For an instant he thought of Shane. Had Shane loved Amber, too? He mentally reviewed the letters he'd memorized. They had been close, no question about that. But he did not think their relationship had blossomed to the point of them falling in love.

And now, there was no chance of that, at all.

For once, the guilt didn't hit. It was hard to feel guilty for being alive. Especially now that he'd realized how much he loved her. With all his heart and soul.

But that didn't mean she felt the same way about him.

Sure, she'd kissed him. But Amber was also young and looking for adventure. For all he knew he was just a nice interlude before she moved to Florida.

He struggled to breathe normally, forcing himself to

shove these tender new feelings aside. No matter how much it hurt, she was in a different place in her life.

He refused to be selfish. To only think about himself. Not anymore.

He'd love Amber enough to let her go.

———

AMBER KNEW guilt was making her more than a little irrational, but she refused to leave the hospital. Bethany would need to stay overnight but would likely be able to come home the following day. That was the good news. The bad news was the way Nick had left without goodbye. She'd thought about calling him, but decided it was better for her to stick close to her family.

Beth had suffered an open tibia fracture. The surgical procedure didn't take long, and when Beth had been returned to her room, her left leg was in a long cast. She made a mental note to get markers so they could draw on it, once the little girl was feeling better.

Andrea tried several times to convince her to go home, but she just couldn't do it. Remembering how she'd purposefully turned her phone off, just to spend time with Nick haunted her. Granted, Andrea had called earlier in the evening, not during the time they'd been watching the drone show. Or kissing as if they'd never stop. Beth had been hit at seven o'clock in the evening. The drone show had not even started until nine. Still, she couldn't seem to separate the fact that she hadn't been there for Andrea and Beth, because she'd been too busy flirting with Nick.

She and Andrea spent the night in Beth's room while their parents watched Ben. Stuart was on his way home from Texas where he was at a sales conference. The doctor released the little girl the following Sunday afternoon. Amber tagged along, to make sure her niece was settled and comfortable. Then she played with Ben so Andrea could prepare something for dinner.

Using his red and blue building blocks, she made a tower, smiling when Ben gleefully swatted it down. As they played, she wondered what Nick was doing. Had he packed up his duffel bag and checked out of The Cozy Inn? Hopped a plane back to Virginia? Did he miss her?

She wished she knew what was going through his mind. But maybe it didn't matter. Nick hadn't called. Time for her to face the truth. He'd probably left town. And really, she couldn't blame him for moving on with his life.

Yet the thought of never seeing him again made her stomach twist and turn like a pretzel.

That night, she didn't sleep well. She woke Monday morning, feeling cranky. She was torn as to whether or not she should plan on giving her notice. It wasn't that she'd changed her mind about leaving Milwaukee, but to go where? That was the question. Despite their fun day at German Fest, she still didn't know how Nick felt. He'd seemed concerned about Beth, but then had left her at the hospital without even stepping in the next day to see how the little girl was doing.

Pushing the irritating thoughts of Nick from her mind, she swiped her badge to clock in and walked down the hall to the rehab unit. She discovered they had a new patient, a young man by the name of Billy Anderson, who had suffered a traumatic leg amputation after an IED explosion. He'd been treated at Walter Reed, the same military hospital Nick had stayed in, but then he'd been transferred here so he could be closer to his family. The ortho surgeon had accepted the initial transfer, then had sent him to their floor for strengthening and general rehab.

"Good morning, Billy. My name is Amber, and I'll be your nurse today."

Silence. Billy lay flat on his back, staring blankly at the ceiling over his head. He acted as if he hadn't heard her.

"You're scheduled to go downstairs for physical therapy at nine. Do you want to shower before or after?"

More silence. The flat expression in his eyes sent alarm bells ringing through her head.

Obviously, Billy was seriously depressed. Worse than the patient who had killed himself after being discharged.

No way, she was not going to allow that to happen to Billy. This young man needed intense psychiatric care.

After explaining she'd be back in an hour, she left. Outside the room, she took a moment to dig a little deeper in his electronic medical record. The orthopedic trauma doc had placed him on antidepressants and, shocker, Roland had even reordered the medication here on rehab. She counted back the days since they'd been started, back when he'd gotten to Walter Reed, then here. Two weeks.

She frowned. The medication either wasn't working or hadn't kicked in yet.

Or Billy was faking swallowing them.

She nibbled her lower lip, wishing Nick were still around. Billy needed someone to talk to, someone like Nick who knew what it was like to suffer a traumatic event. Of course, the young man also needed to be under the care of the psychologists on staff. The only problem was that most of them were older. She couldn't help thinking Billy might respond better to someone younger.

If anyone could get through this young man's stubborn silence, Nick could.

She hoped.

When she returned to the nurse's station, she was surprised to find Dr. Roland seated at a computer, reading a chart.

"Good morning, Dr. Roland." She spoke in a polite tone, although the dark bruises still hadn't faded from her wrist and knee.

"Hrmph." He barely acknowledged her greeting, and he didn't tear his gaze from the screen.

She edged closer, trying to ascertain if there were any smell of alcohol. She didn't smell anything unusual until she was standing right over his shoulder. And even then the odor was faint. So faint she thought maybe she was imagining it.

"Is that Billy's chart? I need to ask you about him." She used the chart as a reason for being so close. Anxiously, she glanced around, looking for some of her colleagues. She didn't want to be the only person who smelled alcohol on the guy. Where was everyone? She couldn't trust her nose to be impartial.

"What about him?" He abruptly turned and scooted his chair backward putting distance between them. The faint scent of alcohol was still there. His brusque attitude didn't soften, as if she was the one who'd wronged him. Not the other way around.

"He's very depressed. I would like our rehab psychiatrist to talk to him sooner, than later."

"Fine. I'll call him." With that, Roland stood and moved to walk around her.

Wait! She almost cried out to stop him from leaving. Then she saw Irene walking down the hallway and hurried over.

"Irene, I need you to go by Roland, tell me if you smell anything funny."

Irene wrinkled her brow. "What do you mean? Why would he smell funny?"

She didn't want to give away her suspicions. "Please? Just go over and ask him a question."

"Okay, fine." Irene turned and headed down the hall. "Dr. Roland? I have a quick question.

She watched as Irene and Roland spoke for a moment before the physician turned away to go into one of the patient's rooms. Irene returned to where she stood.

"Well?" She stared expectantly at her colleague. "What do you think?"

"I don't think anything." Irene shrugged. "There may have been a hint of alcohol on his breath, but it's hard to say for sure. Besides, just because he may have had a little too much to drink last night. That doesn't mean he's impaired."

"You smelled it too?" She blew out a breath in relief. "It's not my imagination, then." It took a moment for the comment to sink in. "Wait a minute. Of course he might be impaired. We are obligated to protect our patients from being cared for by doctors or nurses under the influence. It's part of the nurse's professional code of conduct. We could lose our nursing license if we don't follow through. We must call Leanne."

"Oh, no, don't drag me into this." Irene lifted her hands and backed off. "I didn't smell anything."

Her jaw dropped. What? She had to be kidding. "Irene, this is serious. What if he makes a mistake? Hurts someone? We can't ignore it."

"It's no secret you're leaving. Easy for you to rock the boat. I need this job." Irene's worried gaze bored into her. "I just found out I'm pregnant. I can't afford to get fired. I think he's fine. There's nothing wrong with his medical decisions. And since you're leaving, I don't really see why you care." With one last glance over her shoulder, Irene hurried off.

Amber stared at her retreating figure with a sense of doom. Roland was dangerous, she knew only too well what happened when he had too much to drink. She had the bruises to prove it. But if she couldn't find someone to corroborate her story, she'd be seen as a troublemaker. Leanne had already put a note in her file and required her to take a professional communication class for being rude. And Irene was right, she already had another job lined up in Florida.

Still, it didn't seem right to let this go.

She stood there, torn by indecision. Roland came out of the patient's room and headed toward her. Their gazes locked and in that instant his tiny, smug smile sent a shaft of fury washing over her. He acted as if he knew her days here were numbered and once she was gone, he'd go right back to doing whatever he wanted.

"Excuse me, Dr. Roland. I need to have another word with you." Amber heard the words coming out of her mouth and desperately wanted to call them back. What was she doing?

"Now what?" His smug smile vanished, replaced by intense irritation.

"I need you to come with me and talk to Leanne." She was winging it, because she didn't know what else to do. "There's an issue we need to resolve."

"I'm busy. Tell your boss I'll talk to her later." Roland brushed past her. She was running out of time. Once he left the unit it would be too late.

"No, wait." She raised her voice when he continued to walk away. "Dr. Roland! Have you been drinking?"

Someone on the other side of the nurse's station audibly gasped. But she'd managed to get his attention. He spun around and marched back toward her.

"What did you say?" His voice was deceptively quiet, but the expression in his eyes shot fiery daggers, as if he wanted nothing more than to light a match to her career.

And maybe he would.

She didn't know what to do. No one came to stand beside her, supporting her. The two of them faced each other as if about to embark in a duel. Then, over Roland's shoulder, she saw Nick walking down the hall, leaning heavily on his cane.

Nick wouldn't let this go. She wasn't totally alone here after all. Thrusting her chin toward Roland in defiance, she lifted her chin. "You heard me. I asked you a question. Have you been drinking? Because I smell alcohol on your breath."

When Roland took another step closer, she wanted very badly to turn and run. She expected him to erupt in a fit of rage. But she hadn't anticipated his hand to swing toward her face, cracking loudly across her cheek.

CHAPTER THIRTEEN

Utterly demoralized, Amber stared at Roland as stinging pain blazed across her cheek. Before she could think of anything to say, Nick rushed over.

"That's it, Roland. You've crossed the line. Again!" Nick's eyes widened as he drew close enough to smell him. "I don't believe it! You've been drinking!"

She finally found her voice. "I'm filing a formal complaint with hospital administration and with the Wisconsin Medical Licensing Board." She was glad Nick was there to smell the alcohol on Roland's breath, but she wasn't letting this man get away so easily. This was the second time he'd physically attacked her. "Hospital administration won't take my intent to file assault charges lightly. And I believe the Wisconsin Medical Licensing Board will also take action against you for working under the influence."

"I'll be your witness, Amber." Irene came out from behind the nurse's station to stand beside her. A little late, but she understood Irene's position. Her unborn baby had to come first.

"Good. That makes three of us. I'll be a witness, too." Nick aligned himself with her, placing his body solidly in front of hers as protection. "I suggest you leave, Roland. Right now. You have no business taking care of patients in your condition."

Roland hesitated, then swung away and walked off the unit. She brought a hand up to cover her flaming cheek. "Good riddance," she muttered.

"Here, let's get some ice." Nick's eyes were full of concern as he gently tugged her hand from her face.

"No, I'm fine." She managed a smile. "Oh, and thanks for coming over to support me, Irene."

"I should have come sooner." Her colleague worried her lower lip between her teeth. "You were right, Amber. I'm so sorry."

"Hey, don't worry. I understand." Amber wished she could turn back the clock and forget the whole ugly scene. At least the part where Roland had hauled off and slapped her. Still, she was satisfied Roland would no longer be a threat to his patients. With an effort she thought about what needed to be done. They still had patients to take care of.

"Are you sure you're okay?" Nick's eyes reflected doubt.

"I'm sure. Annoyed, embarrassed and upset more than anything. There are bigger issues to worry about." She thought about her new patient. "Nick, would you do me a favor? I would really like you to go talk to one of my patients."

"Sure. Who?"

"Billy Anderson."

He sighed and took a step back. "I'm not sure my talking to Billy will do any good. That boy needs professional help."

"Yes, I know." There was no arguing that. "But in reviewing his chart, he has had professional help both in the form of medication and psychiatric care. Maybe what he needs is unprofessional help from someone who's been there."

He stood for a long moment, then nodded, his expression resigned. "I can try. What's going on? Did he refuse therapy?"

"He isn't cooperating with therapy, but that's only part of the problem. He's very depressed." She lowered her voice. "Please, just try to talk to him. Make sure he sees he's not alone in this."

"All right." He blew out a breath. "Has psych come to see him yet?"

"No, not today, yet. Roland was just going to call them. I can do that, now." She turned back towards the nurse's station. When she approached, Betty the unit clerk avoided her gaze.

She told herself she didn't care. Even though Roland was in the wrong, it seemed she may still be a *persona non grata* around here. She'd done what she thought was right, but maybe she could have used a more tactful approach.

The phone rang, and Betty turned to look at her. Understanding, she picked up the phone, recognizing the call was from her boss. "Hi Leanne."

"Amber, I understand you're causing a little excitement on the unit." Leanne must have found out about Roland. Probably from Betty. Bad news traveled fast.

"Yes. Dr. Tanner and I both smelled the alcohol on Dr. Roland's breath. And I tried to get him to come off the unit to talk to you in your office, but he refused."

"I heard." Leanne tone was somewhat sympathetic. "I wanted you to know that Dr. Johnson is already aware of the situation. Dr. Roland has been put on medical leave immediately and until further notice."

"Good." She sucked in a breath and then made a quick decision. "Leanne, as long as you're on the phone, I'd like to move up my resignation date. I would ask that my last day be two weeks from today."

There was a long pause as Leanne digested this information. "I see. All right, I'll change your last day of employment with us for two weeks from today. I'm really sorry to see you go."

"I'll miss you, too, Leanne. But thanks." After she hung up the phone, she was hit by an overwhelming sense of relief. At least now she could leave knowing Roland was no longer a threat to their patients. She caught a glimpse of Nick disappearing in Billy's room. She hesitated for a moment, then walked down the hall. Pausing outside the door, she listened to Nick's deep voice, hoping and praying this would work.

"I've been in your shoes—do you want me to prove it?" The rustle of clothing made her eyes widen. Was Nick really stripping down to his skivvies to show Billy his scars?

"So, a few measly scars aren't anything like losing a leg." Billy didn't sound impressed. "It's gone forever."

"Yes, that's true. But tell me this, is a leg that doesn't work any better?" Nick's tone remained calm, logical. "Would you be happier sitting in that chair with two paralyzed legs? Or even one paralyzed leg?"

There was a long moment of silence.

"Look, Billy, I know this is a difficult time. And if you look around, you'll always find people who are better off and worse off than you are. I dealt with the same anger you're feeling right now. It's a normal part of the grieving process. But anger isn't going to change your situation. Action and attitude, will. You need to accept the hand you were dealt and figure out what to do next. Are you going to fold? Or play the game? Are you willing to take another card?" There was a long pause, before Nick said, "Rehab is another card, Billy. It's a chance to get back on your feet, even if one of them is a prosthesis."

Billy remained silent for so long, Amber edged closer, ready to intervene if necessary.

"You really think there's a woman out there who will fall for a guy without a leg?" Billy asked in a low agonized tone.

Oh, Billy. Her heart squeezed in her chest.

"I've worried about the same thing with my scars," Nick said bluntly. "But I've found since my accident that women are better at overlooking our physical limitations than men are." Nick didn't brush off his concern or hand him a line. "Will some women be turned off by it? Yes, probably. I won't lie to you. But I think women need emotional strength from a guy more than anything else. The toughest part is overcoming our own insecurities in order to provide it."

There was another long silence, as Billy digested this information.

"Take the first step. Go to therapy. Once you realize what your life could be like when you are able to wear a prosthesis and walk around on your own two feet, I think you will feel better."

"Alright." Billy's voice was so quiet she could barely hear it. "I'll go to therapy."

Blinking away a stray tear Amber swallowed hard. Billy was taking the first step. It didn't mean there that it would be an easy road for him to take. But she hoped, she prayed, Billy would be one of those who would make it home.

"Good." More rustling as Nick pulled his clothes back on. "And, Billy? I am here if you need to talk."

Amber wanted to linger and to wait for Nick to thank

him, but she had dawdled enough and really needed to see her other patients. Knowing she'd find Nick later, she hurried down the hall.

His words, though, echoed in her mind. *Women need emotional strength from a guy more than anything else. The toughest part is overcoming our insecurities in order to provide it.* Had Nick been referring to the two of them? Hope sprouted like new, green shoots from the depths of her heart.

Maybe, their relationship was more important to him than she'd realized.

NICK LEFT Billy's room to respond to a page from Rick Johnson. He glanced around for Amber, then heard her voice in another patient's room. He wanted to give her an update about Billy agreeing to attend therapy, but he figured he'd better go see what Johnson wanted to talk about.

He left the unit to head toward the administrative offices.

"Rick." Nick nodded at the chief of staff on entering his office. They shook hands. "What can I do for you?"

"Thought you should know, Roland refused to seek treatment for a potential alcohol problem." Rick sat back in his chair and tapped his fingertips together. "Which left me no choice but to terminate him."

It was difficult to summon any sympathy for Roland. Not after the way he'd slapped Amber. "Too bad."

"Yes, actually it is." Rick frowned. "His wife died of cancer two years ago and he hasn't been the same since. I had hoped he'd come around after I gave him the responsibility of being the medical director. Despite everything these past few months, he was once a very good physician."

Oh, man. He rubbed his temple. He hadn't known anything about Roland's wife dying of cancer. And he suspected the nurses on the unit were not aware of it either. Now he did feel sorry for the guy. A little, anyway. "There's still time for him to get help. I'll try to talk to him."

Rick waved that off. "No, I'll talk to him. He's only going to see you as part of the problem. Besides, that's not why I asked you here."

He waited with patient curiosity. He couldn't imagine there was anything else to discuss. Especially since he hadn't yet put in his notice that he was leaving the temporary hospitalist position.

"I spoke with your boss in Fairfax, Virginia." He was surprised Rick's comment. "Steven White is a big fan of yours. But he has some concerns about your ability to return to your previous position."

Opening and closing the fingers on his injured hand, he managed to keep his expression impassive. "He has every reason to be concerned. I won't be able to perform surgery. Ever. Steven is probably waiting for my resignation."

Rick nodded. "That's what I thought. Would you consider staying on here? I have an open medical director position to offer you."

Stunned, he stared at him. "I don't have the credentials to be the medical director of rehabilitation."

"Take the boards, it shouldn't be too hard for a smart guy like you." Rick didn't seem concerned. "With your trauma surgery background, it's not a stretch. With your personal experience, you probably know more about rehab than some of the other physicians do. These past few weeks have convinced me you're perfect for the job."

He didn't know what to do, or what to say. A part of him wanted to run, to get away from facing the truth. He'd always wanted to be a surgeon. Couldn't believe the career he'd loved had been snatched out of his reach.

Yet, how much longer could he continue to fool himself into believing otherwise? The incident with the central line had convinced him his career was finished. And what was that he had told Billy? He wasn't going to fold. Or leave the game. Rick Johnson was offering him a chance to take another card.

The offer of staying did interest him. His chat with Billy hadn't been as awful as he thought it would be. And as the physician in charge of the unit, there were things he could do around here to help. Like pushing to renovate the empty wing to put the rehab gym on the same floor where the patients were.

He warmed to the idea. Why couldn't he take the rehabilitation medicine boards? And staying here would give him a place, a purpose. He'd lived while Shane had died, but his life was worth something. And maybe it was time he found his path. The path God had chosen for him.

What about Amber? She wanted to travel, to see the world, but her family was here. Maybe she would consider staying?

No, that wasn't fair. Amber needed to make her own decisions, and so did he. This decision had to be about him. His life. His career.

"Okay." A sense of rightness swept over him as he accepted the position. "I'll take your offer, Rick. Thank you."

"Great." Johnson grinned. "I've asked Kathy, Roland's former assistant, to clean his personal stuff out of his office so you can move in." He picked up a key from his desk and handed it over. "She'll have the office ready for you within the hour."

Nick closed his injured hand around the key and stood. There was still time to back out, to change his mind, but he knew he wouldn't. "I'll find out when I can take the boards, and of course, I'll have to prepare for them."

"I know you will." Johnson didn't look concerned. "I'm glad you're staying. You'll be a great addition to the rehab medicine team. I think you're going to be an even better medical director."

With a nod, Nick left. In a daze, he returned to the rehab unit. When he saw Billy, seated in his wheelchair, he couldn't help but smile. And when the kid propelled himself down to the elevators for his scheduled session in the physical therapy gym, he knew he'd made the right choice.

For him.

THREE HOURS later Nick was seated in his new office, facing a computer screen full of unopened emails and a pile of paperwork that needed to be taken care of. Apparently, Roland hadn't done much of anything over the past few months.

One item caught his eye. A request for a professional reference from Traveling Nurses, Inc. for staff nurse Amber Monroe.

Kathy poked her head in the door. "I'm sorry to bother you, but I've had several messages from that traveling nurse company. Apparently, they really want that reference."

He stared at the request on the screen. And if he didn't fill it out? Then what? He shook his head. Amber would still go. She'd find someone else to give her professional reference. Besides, this needed to be her choice, not his.

"I'll complete this right now," he promised. He pulled the keyboard close and prepared a glowing reference for Amber.

He emailed it he emailed it and also printed a copy when Kathy called from her desk in the outer office. "Yes?"

"There's a nurse here to see you, Amber Monroe."

His pulse quickened. "Send her in."

She strode through the doorway, looking upset. "I didn't believe it when Leanne told me."

He stood. "It's true."

"You took Roland's job." It was an accusation not a congratulations.

"Yeah, I did."

"But I've already given my notice."

The letter burned in his hand. "I know."

"And that's all you have to say? Don't you care?"

He cared, more than she'd ever know. He loved her. But he couldn't be the reason she stayed, she had to figure out what she wanted from her life by herself. His hopes and dreams broke into tiny little pieces.

"I care, Amber." He willed her to see the truth. "But working with Billy made me realize how right you were. This is my job now, assisting other rehab patients like myself. I can't be the world traveler you need."

"Don't ask me to stay here, because I can't." She spun away, rubbing her hands over her bare arms. "I've never been outside Wisconsin. All my life I've dreamed of traveling—of seeing the world. I have to go somewhere. Anywhere." She whirled back to face him. "I'm happy you've decided to try rehab but you can practice at another hospital. We can go to Virginia. Or somewhere else. I don't care. You pick the place and we'll go."

"I'm not leaving." He recoiled from the anguish he saw reflected in her eyes. In that moment, he realized she really did care for him. Despite his faults and his scars. But he couldn't change himself just to make her happy. And he would never ask her to do that, either. "I've made my decision to stay. But I think you should travel, if that's what you want. I don't blame you for wanting to see a part of the world. I was just like you, once. Looking for adventure. Just make sure you're not going for the wrong reasons."

"What wrong reasons? Because it's always been my dream?" Her tone held an unusual bitterness.

"No. Because you're using your desire to travel as an excuse to escape your family."

"That's not what I am doing at all." She threw up her hands. "Trust me, leaving my family is only an added benefit. The confetti sprinkles on top of my ice cream cone of independence. Traveling is what I've always wanted to do."

The letters she'd written to Shane had stressed that very thing. And he knew she deserved to have this time to herself. To see the world. There was no use trying to talk her out of it, anymore than he'd reconsider his position.

They stood, a wide chasm between them.

With a horrible sense of doom, he handed the letter to her. "I've already emailed this to the traveling nurse company. I wanted to be sure you had a copy as well. You'll be happy to know I gave you a glowing reference. Your job in Florida is waiting for you."

She took the letter from his hand and frowned at it for a long moment. "You wrote me a letter of recommendation?" Her voice was dull, flat. A little too much like Billy's had been. "I thought you cared about me?"

"I do."

"Then how can you ask me to stay?"

"How can you ask me to leave?"

A long, heavy silence fell between them.

He couldn't stand it a minute longer period he forced himself to sound enthused. "Hey, stop looking so grim. You just said this is your dream. I completely understand. You're young and have your whole life ahead of you." He remembered how excitement had hummed through his system when he'd been offered to do his special surgical training program in Beijing. He couldn't steal that thrill from her, now or ever.

He loved her too much.

He stood, helpless to do anything but convince her to go. "I'll be here when you come home for visits. I think you're going to love working in Florida. And I think it's important for you to follow your dream."

CHAPTER FOURTEEN

Florida at the very end of July was suffocatingly hot. Humidity bloated the air and thick dark clouds loomed ominously low on the horizon. Swaying palm trees towered over the dull gray ribbon of highway. Amber peered through the window of the back seat of her rideshare—anxious to wallow in the ambiance of every sight and every sound.

She didn't want to admit her keen disappointment upon discovering that, aside from the scrub brush, palm trees, lack of green grass, and stucco single story houses in bright colors, there wasn't much to distinguish Fort Meyers, Florida from Milwaukee. With an irritated sigh, she shoved the thought aside. There were plenty of different experiences waiting for her. People, for one. Her rideshare driver, a huge guy with deadlocks who loved to chat, and spoke with a decidedly Jamaican accent, was a perfect example. There were pawn shops on every corner, something she'd never seen before. She was certain that if she tried, she'd find all kinds of excitement here.

Like the impending storm. They had summer thunderstorms in Milwaukee too, but not during the past few weeks as they'd suffered a severe drought. She was certain storms here were more impressive, especially watching them roll in off the ocean. She leaned forward to get the rideshare driver's attention. "Does it rain here often?"

"Every day."

Her eyes widened in horror. A white smile flashed in his dark face.

"It's our rainy season. The day generally starts out fair and sunny, but every afternoon the storm clouds move in off the ocean and we get a nasty rainstorm. But the weather blows over in a few hours."

"How long is the rainy season?"

The guy shrugged and then shouted, "Hey!" He leaned on his horn when someone started to move into his lane. She tugged on her seat belt to ensure it was secure. The drivers down here seemed a little more reckless then back home. Lightning ripped across the sky. Booming thunder followed several seconds later.

"Depends," he said, continuing their conversation. "But September through November is the height of our hurricane season."

Oh. Great. She sank back into her seat with a weak smile. Hurricane season. Of course. She vaguely remembered hearing about that when she'd signed up for this assignment. Living through a hurricane would be exciting.

Maybe.

She did her best to summon some enthusiasm. At least she was here, in Fort Meyers, Florida. Her boxes of belongings scheduled to arrive in the next couple of days. She couldn't wait to unpack. Her first plane ride had been uneventful, but she'd gripped the seat arms tight as they'd taken off because her mind conjured images of Nick and Shane's plane crash.

Nick. Her chest tightened, stinging with shards of regret. She hadn't seen him in over two weeks. The hospital grapevine indicated that he had left to take care of his own move from Virginia to Wisconsin. While he'd been gone, she'd hopped a plane headed in the complete opposite direction.

She'd honestly believed he'd cared for her. Maybe even had started to fall in love with her. The way she had fallen in love with him. Right before he had written a glowing letter of recommendation on her behalf and encouraged her to leave.

What a fool she'd been. A guy like Nick could have any woman he wanted. A few shared kisses didn't mean anything.

The driver pulled into the driveway leading to her condo complex. Fat drops of rain splattered on the windshield.

"Thanks so much." Using the app on her phone she paid and tipped the man, then jumped out, dragging the single carry on suitcase behind her. One step later, the sky opened up and dumped buckets of water onto her head.

Rats. Ducking her face to avoid the water, she ran up to the second story condo doorway awkwardly carrying her suitcase, and crowded as close to the door as she could to get away from the slanting rain. Not that it mattered. Her clothes were already plastered to her skin.

Inside, the air smelled stale and musty. Despite the heat, she opened the windows a few inches, to air the place out, then glanced around her new home.

A plethora of seashells decorated the walls and dotted the expanse of the polyester bedspreads. The neutral earth tones and endless beach motif was nice enough. Maybe once she'd earned her first paycheck, she'd go shopping and pick out some things in bright bold colors. And once her belongings arrived, and the pictures of her family would make the place feel more like home.

Thoughts of her family had her glancing at the screen on her cell phone. Any minute she expected to see a slew of messages from her parents, her brothers, and Andrea.

But there wasn't a single one. Her shoulders slumped as she sank down on the edge of the bed. Okay, she could admit this was a slow start and the rain pelting on her windows didn't help her dismal mood. There was no reason to sit here and second guess her decision. She hadn't even given her new home a fair chance.

She decided against calling her family. Wasn't this what she'd wanted? To be left alone. To be independent. To follow her dream of exploring the world, one traveling nurse assignment after another.

Alone.

The word had never sounded so pitiful.

NICK WATCHED Billy work in the physical therapy gym with a sense of satisfaction. The kid was really coming along. Between therapy and psychiatric support, the young man was doing better. He worked with the equipment as if he were on a mission to get out of there.

The exact same way he had. Those months he'd spent in rehab had been the longest of his life. And it was oddly comforting to help others along the same road he'd taken.

He returned to his office and the endless work awaiting his attention. One thing he'd discovered, a medical director position involved far more paperwork and emails than he'd ever dreamed possible.

Sinking into his chair, he wondered about Amber. How was she doing? Did she love sunny Florida? Had she already started her new job?

Did she miss him as much as he missed her?

He dropped his head into his hands and squeezed his temples to ease the dull ache. Sending her away had been the right thing to do, but he couldn't stand the thought that she might hate him for it. Although surprisingly, she hadn't resented him for the part he'd unwittingly played in Shane's death. Maybe she could forgive him for this too?

What if she wasn't happy? He lifted his head to stare out the window. He knew a big part of her leaving had to do with escaping the perceived claustrophobia of her family. Maybe she was miserable without them.

Or maybe that was just wishful thinking on his part.

Nick leaned forward and began reading emails. There were several medical staff policies needing his review. He'd made his choice and she'd made hers. He needed to remember that.

———

"WHAT HAPPENED TO DR. ROLAND, your medical director?" A little over two weeks later, Amber found herself seated across from Charlotte, her new boss at Lee County hospital. She'd already completed the basic orientation. Thankfully the care was very similar to what she was accustomed to. Charlotte had wanted a one-on-one update before releasing her from orientation, to a full-fledged staff member status.

"According to this letter he was recently replaced by a Dr. Tanner."

"Yes." She fidgeted in her seat. She didn't want to go

into detail, but worried the woman would disregard Nick's letter if she didn't explain. "Unfortunately, Dr. Roland had some personal problems, which began to interfere with the medical care he was providing to our patients. I had no choice but to report him to Hospital Administration and the Wisconsin State Licensing Board. As a result, our chief of staff asked for Dr. Roland's resignation."

"Really?" Charlotte's eyes rounded. "I'm sure it wasn't easy for you to report him to the state medical board. Wow. You've had quite an interesting career."

Seeing her life through the eyes of a stranger made her sit up straighter in her chair. She'd never considered everything that had gone on with Dr. Roland as interesting or exciting. Yet there was no mistaking the awed expression in Charlotte's eyes. Her boss probably wouldn't look so impressed if she'd heard how Roland had slapped her. She resisted the urge to cover her cheek.

After a few minutes of chitchat, Charlotte sent Amber an electronic copy of her schedule. Once the meeting was over, she left. But Charlotte's words followed her on the walk home. Had she been so intent on seeking excitement that she hadn't recognized the experience when it had smacked her in the face? Like literally? Nagging doubt assailed her and her footsteps slowed.

Could Nick be right? Was she so busy trying to escape from her overprotective family that she used traveling as an excuse to avoid dealing with them? Had she really let Alec annoy her so much she'd moved over a thousand miles from home?

Leaving Nick behind?

A loud crash from the open door of a restaurant diverted her attention from her thoughts. "Help! This man needs help!"

Without hesitation, she scurried inside. She blinked, forcing her eyes to adjust to the dimly lit room. "What is it? What's wrong?"

"I think he's having a heart attack!" A skinny guy with long gray hair pulled back in a ponytail and wearing a chocolate smeared apron wrung his hands in dismay.

She dropped to her knees beside a large, chalky faced man who looked too young to be suffering from a heart attack. He sat on the floor in a daze, surrounded by remnants of broken plates and saucers.

"Sir? Can you tell me what happened?" She checked his pulse, not surprised to find it was clipping along at a rapid pace. His skin was clammy and diaphoretic. Regardless of how young he appeared to be, she suspected he really was having a myocardial infarction.

"Feels like... I can't get... my breath. My chest...too tight."

"Call 911 and get me a baby aspirin." Too bad she didn't have any nitroglycerin tablets with her. Or an oxygen tank. Or even her stethoscope. The skinny man in the apron dug out his cell phone.

"I want you to sit here and try to relax." Not an easy task, she certainly understood. She tried to calm her own racing heart. "I'm a nurse. You'll find it easier to get your breath if you just close your eyes for a minute and try to relax." She hoped her smile was reassuring. "What's your name?"

"Darrin."

"My name is Amber. I'm going to stay here with you until the ambulance arrives."

Darrin's hopeful expression crumbled. "Ambulance? Am I that sick?"

"I don't have any baby aspirin." The guy with the ponytail had finished his 911 call and now returned from the kitchen. "I have regular aspirin."

"That will work fine. We'll cut it in half." She tried to reassure him, too. If ponytail guy fell apart, she'd have two patients on her hands. "Will you please get a glass of water?"

He nodded and darted back to the kitchen.

She managed to maintain control of the situation until the screeching of sirens filled the air. As the noise grew louder, Darrin's heart rate shot up dramatically.

"Relax, Darrin, slow your breathing. The faster you breathe, the more oxygen your body needs. And that means less oxygen for your heart." She couldn't lose him now when help was near. "Look at me, Darrin. I'm right here. I won't leave you. You're doing fine."

Darrin's eyes clung to hers, as he struggled to slow his breathing.

She repeated soothing words while the sirens halted outside the open door. Laden with equipment, the EMT's rushed in.

Thankful for the additional help, she held on to Darrin's hand and explained what had happened. "His pulse is tacky at 126 and his respirations are 30 and shallow. He's been extremely diaphoretic and I've given him half a regular aspirin."

"Good work." The EMT closest to her was about her age and extremely handsome with his beach blonde looks and dark tan. She didn't feel one iota of attraction when he flashed her a very interested smile while looping oxygen tubing over Darrin's ears and inserting the prongs in his nose. "Why don't you come along with us during the rest of our shift? We could use the help."

She gave him a tense smile. "No, thanks, I just started a

new job at Lee County hospital." She took the leads from the other EMT 's and placed them on Darrin's chest. "These are so that we can see what's going on with your heart," she explained.

"Okay." Darrin clutched her hand as soon as she'd finished.

The beach blonde paramedic deftly started an IV in Darrin's arm. Once he had the fluid running, he pretended to sigh. "Lee County, huh? Tell me your name and I'll look you up. We make runs there fairly often."

She didn't answer, her brief moment of humor fading into annoyance with his persistence in flirting with her when they had a patient to take care of. She held her patient's gaze. "Darrin, listen, can you hear your heartbeat on the monitor? Hear how strong the beats are?"

He nodded, his eyes wide.

"You're doing just fine," she reassured him.

Moments later, the EMT's had Darrin safely tucked onto the gurney. She held the man's hand until the point where they slid him into the back of the ambulance. The beach blonde EMT shot her one last sexy smile before closing the doors behind him.

"Is he gonna be alright?" The ponytailed man asked from behind her.

"I'm sure he'll be fine. You can call the hospital in a little while to check on him." She glanced at the mess on the floor. "Looks like you will need someone to cover the rest of his shift.

"Yeah, well, I just hope Darrin is okay."

She smiled. "Me too."

After leaving the restaurant, she continued toward her condo. But the delay with Darrin had given the dark storm clouds a head start. There was a streak of lightning, followed by a deep warning rumble of thunder. The usual four in the afternoon rain storm was upon her.

Her spirits sank. *Don't rain, don't rain.* She picked up her pace, jogging despite the suffocating heat. At least she still wore her hospital scrubs and tennis shoes.

The deluge of rain hit when she was still several blocks from her condo. She continued running, the water hitting so hard she could barely see, especially with her hair plastered to her face.

When she dashed up the stairs to her second floor condo, she saw the dark looming shape a moment too late. She plowed against a distinctly male form.

Not the blonde EMT? For a moment panic flared, and she was about to fight him off, until a familiar scent teased her senses and a pair of strong hands wrapped around her arms.

"Amber? Are you alright?"

"Nick?" She shoved her wet hair from her eyes. Could she have looked any less attractive? This was not how she'd anticipated seeing him again. "What are you doing here?"

"Waiting for you." He pulled her close to give her a quick hug, despite her soaked scrubs. "Do you have your key? Let's get inside. You need to dry off so you won't get sick."

Strangled laugh caught in her throat. "I've been caught in the rain so much I don't know what dry is. It's always raining shortly after the end of my shift." Still, she dug in her pocket for her key and then unlock the door. Stepping across the threshold, she waved a hand. "Have a seat, I'll be right back." She ducked into her bedroom and hastily stripped out of her wet clothes and toweled herself dry. Why had he come? Did he have news from home?

Bad news?

Throwing on a clean pair of shorts and a tank top, she shot back into the living area. "Is something wrong? My parents? Alec? Beth?"

Nick held up a hand. "Nothing is wrong. Your family is fine, Amber. They send their love."

"Thank goodness." She let out a deep breath. "For a moment I thought... well, never mind." Feeling awkward she ran her fingers through her wet hair. "I'm really surprised to see you."

Nick looked wonderful. Not as classically handsome as the beach blonde EMT, but her pulse skipped a beat when he held her gaze. The sizzling chemistry that always shimmered between them, had not lessened one bit.

"I needed to see you." Nick's smile was wistful. "I miss you."

"Oh, Nick." She threw herself into his arms. "I miss you, too."

"Amber, I know how much you want to travel." He spoke in a low voice as he held her close. "But I can't stop thinking about you. My life isn't the same without you."

"I've discovered traveling isn't very much fun when you're all alone." Her words were muffled against his chest.

There was a long pause, then he gently pulled away. "Hey, I didn't mean to get all maudlin. How's your new job? I have a lot to tell you. I've gotten approval for relocating the physical therapy gym to the second floor. Will you come and see it on your next visit back?"

She stared at him, the abrupt change in subject catching her off guard. But then she understood. He thought she was asking him to leave his job to travel with her. Which wasn't as easy as it sounded. In truth, there were not as many temporary physician positions as there were nursing ones. She wet her dry lips. "Of course, I will, but first I need to explain something to you. Remember what you said about making sure I was leaving for the right reasons?"

He nodded, his gaze intense.

"You were right. I was running from my family. I love them dearly, but they were making me so crazy. Especially Alec, who sees drug dealers on every corner." She dropped her gaze to the carpet then forced yourself to look up at him. "But you know what? I figured out while I've been here that I can be independent and remain close to home. I stood up to Roland, didn't I?"

"Are you saying what I think you're saying?" Nick asked.

She laughed. "I think so. I've committed to stay three months. I can't back out of my contract. When my commitment is up, I can leave. I can return home. I love my family and I know they love me. I was stupid to use traveling as an excuse to run away."

"It's not stupid." His smile was crooked. "I know what it's like to want to see the world. I did that myself. And really enjoyed the fabulous places I've been. You deserve that chance. I can't be the one who takes that from you."

"I don't think I need to travel non-stop." She realized how stupid it was to have even thought she could do that. Seeing the world paled compared to spending time with Nick. "I need to tell you something else," she said in a low voice.

"I love you," Nick said.

Her eyes widened, and then she laughed. "I love you too." She tipped her head to the side. "I have a feeling we can rack up a few frequent flyer miles during the next three months."

"I love that idea." His smile faded. "I know you're young

and you have your whole future ahead of you, but—will you please marry me?"

"Yes, I'll marry you. We both have our whole lives ahead of us, not just me. When are you going to figure that out?"

"When I have a wedding ring safely secured on your finger." He pulled her into his arms. "You won't regret this, Amber. I promise. I love you. More than you'll ever know."

Her heart soared at his declaration. "I love you, too."

"I'll take you any place in the whole world for our honeymoon," he continued earnestly. "You name the spot."

"Hmm." She pretended to think. "We should choose a place neither of us has been to before. How about Bora Bora?" She wrapped her arms around his neck and pulled him down for a kiss as giddy happiness swelled in her heart. A few minutes later, she leaned back and looked up at him. "I was kidding, you know. It doesn't matter where we go. As long as we're together. And as long as we always return home."

"I like the sound of that," he murmured. Then kissed her again, making her hope the next three months would go by, very fast.

I HOPE you enjoyed Amber and Nick's story in *Broken Dreams*. Are you ready for Alec and Jillian's story in *Crushed Promise*? Click here!

DEAR READER

Over twenty years ago I wrote a short series about the Monroe family. I've recently updated these stories and have decided to re-issue them now. I realize these are not my typical Christian romantic suspense books but I hope you enjoy them anyway. Alec's story will be available soon, then Adam's story and finally Austin's story. I hope you give the rest of the Monroe books a try.

Anyone choosing to purchase eBooks or audiobooks directly from my website will receive a 15% discount by using the code **LauraScott15**. I usually have the Finnegan books available there, first, before they are released on other vendor sites.

I adore hearing from my readers! I can be found through my website at https://www.laurascottbooks.com, via Facebook at https://www.facebook.com/LauraScott Books, Instagram at https://www.instagram.com/laurascott books/, and Twitter https://twitter.com/laurascottbooks. Also, take a moment to sign up for my monthly newsletter to learn about my new book releases! All subscribers receive a free novella not available for purchase on any platform.

Until next time,

Laura Scott

P.S. Read on for a sneak peek of *Crushed Promise*.

CRUSHED PROMISES

Chapter One

Dr. Jillian Davis kept her head high, hopefully portraying a confidence she didn't feel as she strode through the emergency department at Trinity Medical Center.

"You're late." Dr.Wayne Netter, one of her colleagues, glared at her from his arrogant stance behind the arena nurse's station.

She ignored him, refusing to explain she was late because her MRI scan had been delayed. Her personal problems were none of his business. Impervious to his glare, she eyed the list of patients displayed on the electronic census board. "I see we have a full house."

"There are a couple of trauma victims on the way in," Lacy, the charge nurse, piped up. "Multiple gunshot wounds. ETA less than two minutes."

"Maybe I should stick around, in case you need help." Wayne Netter suffered from delusions of grandeur, acting as if he was the backbone of the emergency department, which is why he could barely tolerate knowing Jillian had been chosen for the role of interim medical director over him.

She raised a brow. "Sure, if you like. Although it's Friday night, and I wouldn't want you to hold up your plans."

Wayne's gaze narrowed and she imagined he was internally debating with himself. Was it more important she believed he had big plans on a Friday night or that she needed his dubious expertise for two simultaneous trauma victims?

Decisions, decisions. She fought a smile, especially when Lacy comically rolled her eyes from behind Wayne's back. Neither of them particularly cared for the guy.

Clearing her throat, she turned her attention to Lacy. "Any other patient care issues I need to know about?"

"Nope." Lacy shot a quick glance at Dr. Netter and Jillian belatedly realized Wayne might take her innocent remark as something derogatory. As if there couldn't possibly be problems while Netter was in charge. She stifled a sigh as Lacy hastened to reassure her, "Everything's fine. Hospital beds are still pretty full and we have a few patients waiting on discharges upstairs."

"Great. I'll head over to the trauma room, then." Jillian walked away, feeling Wayne's piercing gaze boring into her back. To make a bad situation worse, she'd also once turned down his offer to go out for dinner, and he'd been impossible to deal with ever since. He just couldn't believe she wasn't interested. As if he were the ED's most eligible bachelor. Of course, he didn't realize she hadn't dated many men in her lifetime. At first because her mother had been ill and later because she just hadn't found anyone interesting enough.

Wayne did not come close to tempting her. When he

didn't follow her into the trauma room, she figured he'd decided not to stick around.

Breathing a sigh of relief, she focused her attention on the nurses and techs scurrying around to prepare the rooms for the incoming trauma patients. Sirens wailed from the ambulance bay and moments later the double doors burst open, spewing chaos into the room.

"Anchor Doe, male, approximately sixteen-years-old with a gunshot wound to the belly, normal saline running wide open through two antecubital peripheral lines." A paramedic called out the pertinent information as the patient was wheeled into the first trauma bay.

"Evergreen Doe, male approximately the same age at sixteen was shot in the chest. We intubated him in the field, but his vitals are deteriorating rapidly. Fluids going wide open through two peripheral antecubital IVs."

Of the two unknown males, identified by names other than John Doe since that became far too confusing in dealing with multiple victims, Evergreen Doe with the chest wound was by far the most serious and required immediate attention. Jillian raised her voice to be heard over the din. "Call for a cardiovascular surgery consult, STAT."

"We already did, when the first call about a gunshot wound to the chest came in," Bonnie, one of the trauma nurses, quickly explained. "They were finishing up in surgery and planned to send a surgeon down."

"I don't see anyone yet. Call them again," Jillian ordered.

A nurse stepped away from the bedside using her hands free phone to make the call.

"Blood pressure barely 70 systolic and heart rate irregular and tacky at 120," Bonnie called out. "Looks like he may be trying to go into a wide complex cardiac rhythm."

Jillian wasn't surprised to see one of the paramedics kneeling on the gurney beside Evergreen Doe, keeping pressure on his chest wound. As the trauma nurses fell into their respective roles on each side of the gurney, she donned sterile gloves and moved closer to examine the severity of the wound.

"Thanks, I have it now." She nodded, indicating he could let up on the wound. A flash of silver on a badge caught her eye and belatedly she realized the man holding pressure wasn't a paramedic at all but a cop.

He released pressure and immediately blood pooled in the center of the young man's chest. The cop slammed his hands back down, covering the gaping wound and leaning his weight over the area. "He's going to bleed to death before the surgeon gets here!"

Jillian couldn't argue—the brief glimpse she'd had of the injury told her it was bad. Really bad. She snapped out orders. "I want four units of O negative blood running through both IV's for a total of eight units, using the rapid infuser. Get this kid's blood pressure up before we lose him. I also want suction here so I can examine this wound."

Marianne, another nurse, reached up and connected a long clear tubing from the wall suction machine, then handed her the other end. Grabbing a pack of sterile gauze off the instrument table, Jillian turned back to the patient. She glanced up at the cop, registering a flash of recognition as she met his intense dark green eyes. "Let up on the wound again and this time stay back."

With a grim expression, he nodded.

When he lifted his hands she shoved the sterile end of the suction catheter into the area to clear most of the blood. Using the gauze to soak up the remaining blood, she examined the wound.

"The bullet has torn through the pericardial sack and injured his heart." The injury to the boy's chest was bad, but he had youth on his side. The young could survive a lot more than your average older adult. "Where is the surgeon?"

"He's on the way," Bonnie responded.

"Blood pressure continuing to drop despite the blood transfusions," Marianne informed her in a terse tone. "We'll need to start CPR."

"Give me another minute." Jillian continued suctioning the blood from the wound, and then carefully packed the area with gauze hoping to buy this kid a little more time.

"Dr. Raymond from CT surgery is here," Bonnie announced.

Finally.

"We've lost his pressure!" Marianne shoved the IV pole aside to reach for the Ambu bag on the wall behind her.

No! Jillian stared at the monitor then glanced down at the young man. "Start CPR."

The cop still kneeling on the gurney placed his hands over the center of the kid's chest and began giving chest compressions. Blood continued to seep from the wound. She didn't waste time telling him to get down—for one thing the strength of his compressions were better than most, and for another, if they didn't fix the hole in this kid's heart soon, their efforts would be futile anyway.

"A bullet punctured the pericardial sac and grazed his myocardium." Jillian quickly gave Raymond the details. "He'll need to go to the OR."

Todd Raymond shook his head as he glanced at the vital signs displayed on the heart monitor. "It's no use. He won't make it to the OR, he's lost too much blood."

Jillian couldn't believe his cavalier attitude. Was he

really going to give up that easily? She held onto her temper with an effort. "Are you telling me you're not even going to try?"

He shrugged. "What do you want me to do—open his chest here?"

"Get the chest tray STAT!" Jillian knew their efforts might be useless but this kid was a teenager, for Pete's sake. Didn't this child deserve every chance possible?

When the tray was open and ready, the cop stopped giving compressions and jumped down from the gurney, knowing without being told that his assistance was no longer needed.

The alarm on the monitor overhead beeped loudly as the kid's heart rhythm went straight line without the aid of having CPR. Jillian wasn't a surgeon but she didn't flinch when Todd drew his scalpel down the center of the boy's chest, meeting up with the open area left by the bullet. "Hand me the Macmillan forceps," Todd said as he opened the ribs to expect the damage to the boy's heart.

She did as he asked, but at that moment the fingers of her right hand went numb and tingly, causing her to drop them. For a split second her horrified gaze met the cops. Good thing the forceps had dropped onto the sterile field. She quickly picked them up again and handed them to Raymond.

"His left ventricle is severely damaged," Todd muttered as he used the forceps to trace the path of the bullet. Jillian crammed more gauze into the blood-filled cavity. "The left lung is also a mess—the bullet tore through the upper lobe."

"Try open heart massage," Jillian said urgently. "Maybe if we can get his blood circulating long enough to get him on the heart lung bypass machine..." She didn't finish. Even she understood that likely wasn't possible. But it would not be for lack of trying.

Todd Raymond did as she asked and messaged the heart, coaxing it back into some semblance of normal function. But even as they all stared at the straight line where the heart rhythm should have been on the monitor, she knew it was too late.

"It's over." Todd removed his hands from the kid's chest, and turned away. "I'm sorry. But with the injuries he sustained, his chance of survival was less than five percent."

He wasn't a percentage, he was a child! She wanted to scream, rant and rave at the tragic death but held herself in check. This boy wasn't the first patient she'd lost and unfortunately, she doubted he would be the last. She opened and closed the fingers of her right hand, trying to shake off the strange tingly sensation. "Thanks for coming down, Todd."

"Sure." The surgeon stripped off his bloody gown and gloves, tossed them in a red trash bag and left.

Jillian removed her bloody gloves too, then forced herself to turn her attention to the team of personnel working over Anchor Doe, the first victim. She'd left her senior resident in charge, using his expertise on the sicker of the two patients. "How are things going, Jack?"

"Fine. He's stable. The trauma surgery team is taking him to the OR to repair the damage to his intestines." Jack Dempsey seemed to have everything under control as she watched the surgical residents packed up the gurney and wheeled Anchor Doe away.

Good. At least they hadn't lost both of them. Losing one young man was bad enough.

When she turned back to Evergreen Doe, she saw the cop still standing there, staring down at the kid, seemingly unaware of the nurses who are cleaning equipment out of the way.

When Marianne moved to pick up the remnants of the boy's bloody shirt and pants, the cop glanced up and held out his hand. "I'll take those."

Marianne glanced at Jillian for confirmation. She nodded, granting her permission. Their policy was always to cooperate with law enforcement when they accompanied a patient to the emergency department. Gunshot and knife wounds were an automatic report to the police, and they had the right to secure evidence of a crime. Marianne dropped the bloody clothes in a plastic bag and handed them over. He took the bag absently, staring at the boy, not appearing to be in a huge hurry to leave.

Now that the worst of the emergency was over, she cast through her memory for the cop's name. Alex? No, Alec. That's right. Alec Monroe. He'd come in about two months ago with a serious knife wound slashed diagonally across his flank requiring a good twenty stitches.

Embarrassed at how she remembered his name over the dozens of other patients she treated over the past few weeks, she wished she could slink away, especially knowing he'd taken note of the way she'd dropped the forceps. Did he wonder what was wrong with her? Or had he attributed the action to pure clumsiness?

"Thanks for going above and beyond with him," Alec said in a low tone, still gazing at the dead boy.

She nodded. "I'm sorry we couldn't do more."

He raised his gaze to hers, and her heart fluttered stupidly in her chest when she noticed he'd recognized her as well. His mouth quirked in half-hearted smile. "Not your fault, Dr. Davis. He had the best doctor in the state as far as I'm concerned."

She felt her cheeks grow warm and inwardly cursed her fair skin. The cop had made her blush two months ago too, teasing her as she'd stitched his wound. He was tall, well over six feet, and wore his chocolate brown hair long and shaggy. She remembered his body was pure solid muscle. She'd been more aware of him than had been proper when taking care of a patient.

Opening and closing her hand again, she fought to maintain her professionalism. "I hope your wound is all healed."

"Sure." His smile disappeared. "I only wish these two kids had tried to settle their dispute with a knife instead of a gun. Then this kid might have had a chance."

"I know." She understood what he was saying. Once she would have argued that violence was violence regardless of the weapon of choice. But the crime rate in Milwaukee, Wisconsin had been climbing over the past few years and so had the use of guns. As a result, they treated more and more victims of gunshot wounds, many of them fatal.

Like this poor boy.

"Thanks again, Dr. Davis." Alec flashed a crooked smile.

Call me Jillian. She almost said the words out loud, but managed to bite them back. She gave a brief nod instead. "Anytime."

Alec turned away, stripping off his bloody gloves and taking a moment to wash his hands in the sink before heading for the door. Jillian watched him walk away, hoping she wouldn't have a reason to see him as a patient in the emergency department anytime soon.

Cops like Alec put their lives on the line every day just to protect the innocent. To protect the public. To protect people like her.

She couldn't imagine a more thankless job.

Or a more dangerous one.

Yet from the little she'd seen of Alec between this visit and the previous one where he'd been cut with a knife, he seemed to thrive on his role, throwing his whole heart and soul into his career. Not many cops would have held pressure on a bleeding chest wound like he had.

Jillian shrugged off her troubled thoughts. Tucking her hands into the pockets of her lab coat, she spun on her heel to head back to the main area of the emergency department. No reason to worry about Alec—she had enough problems of her own.

Like how long would she have to wait to hear the results of her MRI?

And did she even want to hear the results?

Her gut instinct shouted no, even though she knew it was better to find out the truth now so she could figure out the potential impact to her career. Her stomach clenched in fear. She knew first hand, after caring for her mother, just how badly this could affect her future. Although likely not for years yet.

Small comfort.

"Dr Davis?"

Surprised, she glanced over her shoulder. A deep frown furrowed Alec's forehead as he strode back toward her.

Yes?" She pivoted and waited for him to reach her.

"Do you have a minute?" His eyes, the color of jade, mesmerized her.

Her heart thudded in her chest. She should say no because, heaven knew, the area was full of patients who might need her attention. But she found herself nodding her consent. "Of course. Is something wrong?"

"You could say that. I pulled these out of the kid's pants

pocket." Alec 's mouth thinned in a grim line as he held the item up for her to see.

"Percocet?" She frowned when she saw the four individually wrapped packages of narcotics. "Was he recently hospitalized?"

Alec cocked his head questioningly. "I don't know. If he was, do medications come individually wrapped like this when you fill a prescription?"

"No." The implication of what he was saying hit her with the force of a ton of bricks. "You're saying these were stolen. Like from a hospital or a clinic."

"Yes." His gaze didn't waver from hers. "Would you know if anyone around here or anywhere else recently reported missing narcotics?"

Jillian opened her mouth and then closed it again without saying anything. Because the answer was yes. Less than a week ago, twelve Percocet tablets, just like the kind Alec held in his hand, had been discovered missing from the locked narcotic drawer right here in the Trinity medical center's emergency department.